Red
Moon
Rising

Best Wishes &
Please enjoy!

Tillie

Red Moon Rising

by

Vickie Mason Randalls

ISBN: 1-55517-467-1
V.1

Published by Bonneville Books

Distributed by:
925 North Main, Springville, UT 84663 • 801/489-4084

CFI

Publishing and
Distribution Since 1986

Cedar Fort, Incorporated
CFI Distribution • CFI Books • Council Press • Bonneville Books

Typeset by Virginia Reeder
Cover design by Adam Ford
Cover design © 2001 by Adam Ford

Printed in the United States of America

Acknowledgments

Thanks to Dee Dee Henry who spent hours with me when I first endeavored to write a book.

James Gates who pored over this first draft and edited as only a friend would do.

Especially my love, David, who waited and hoped, listened and listened again, and always believed in me.

Jesi, Davey and Rocky who willingly gave up their Mom while she wrote. They were always the best critics.

To all my friends and family who kept saying, "it's really good" and "you can do it."

To Lee Nelson, my editor, who read my book and said those two magical words that made it all worth it—"Well-written."

To Granny who made it possible for me to go to college in the first place, who turned early mother-hood into a joy for me and the kids. Happy 88th!

And last, my Dad, who first taught me how to love and to Mama, who lost to cancer in death, but won by the way she lived...I'll see you again on That Great Day.

And I will shew wonders in the heavens and in the earth, blood, and fire, and pillars of smoke.

The sun shall be turned into darkness, and the moon into blood, before the great and the terrible day of the Lord come.

(Joel 2:30-31)

Chapter 1
Sometime In The Near Future

The arrow whizzed by with such ferocity that Rachel grabbed both her ears and pressed hard against the odd tickle that spiraled through her head. When the sensation had subsided somewhat, she raised her head slightly and looked toward the arrow's origin. From her position on the ground it was hard to see anything except the steady rolling of the dust.

After crawling to a fallen tree, Rachel lay very still, listening. All she could hear was the frantic pounding of her own heart. Where were the others? She had only raised her head an inch or two above the dust line when the second arrow sped by. Only seconds passed before strong arms snatched her from the ground and carried her purposefully in the opposite direction.

Rachel tried to pull away. She kicked and jerked with all of her might, but the arms were like steel bands around her, strapping her arms to her sides. Suddenly they stopped and she heard a male voice whisper near her ear, "If you promise to calm down, I won't have to tie you up like the others."

Glancing in the direction of his gesture, Rachel saw the rest of her band, hands tied, face down in the dirt. All except Sarah, who just stood there, her shirt front torn, looking miserable and humiliated. With that scene before her, Rachel simply lost all reason and brought her foot down hard along her enemy's shin.

The male howled in pain, and though she hadn't believed it possible, he increased his grip. After a few brief moments of futile struggle, Rachel slumped in exhaustion against her captor.

"Do I tie you or not?" came the voice again, surprisingly in a calm whisper against her ear.

"I can't...breathe," was all Rachel could squeeze from her nearly collapsed lungs.

He dropped her as quickly as he had snatched her up, so Rachel fell to the ground with a thud, gasping for some of the dust-filled air. Sarah ran to Rachel and began thumping her on the back.

"Sarah! Would...you stop that! You're...beatin' what little air I have left in me...out."

Rachel's younger sister stopped her thumping and looked at Rachel in a dazed stare for several long seconds before nodding numbly. Her green eyes brimmed with tears she was trying desperately to hold back.

Lowering her voice so that only Sarah could hear her, Rachel hissed, "If you bawl like a baby, now, I'm gonna be the one hurtin' you!"

Satisfied that her sister had been properly reprimanded for her shameful cowardice, Rachel turned her fierce glare toward the man who had her entire band captured. It dawned on her that this male was sparing her being tied because she was a female. As ridiculous as the notion was, she decided to use his weakness against him.

"You big bull! You've scared my sister to death and now she's cryin'. What did you do to her?" Rachel stood with both hands on her hips waiting for an answer.

To Rachel's extreme amusement, the big bull grabbed his jacket off and gingerly handed it to Sarah to cover herself.

"Nothing! Well, except to detain her. It was necessary," he defended. "I'm sorry we've inconvenienced you and your sister, but this is the third time your group has disabled the union. It was time we had a talk." The tall man with long dark hair looked sincere and threw another concerned glance toward Sarah.

Interesting, thought Rachel. A man with a conscience. "This don't look like talk to me," retorted Rachel, throwing her own concerned glance toward the four male members of her band still lying in the dirt.

"We tried to talk, but that one," the bull pointed toward the small, dark-haired man on the ground, "tried to stick a knife in my back. That's when we decided to do it this way." He glanced with some satisfaction toward the spectacle of the four roughnecks subdued in the dirt.

The *we* part caused Rachel to look around since the bull was the only one in sight, so she simply stated what was on her mind. "Who's the *we*, anyhow? We ain't never all been caught like this before. How'd you do it?"

Two others walked from the trees as if on cue, another male and a female. They were younger than the bull and looked harmless. The male slapped the bull on the back and said, "See, I told you there were only six of them." He grinned and continued, "But you never trust your little brother, huh?"

The bull gave him a tolerant look and then addressed Rachel's unanswered question. "We had a lot of help beyond our own. It's important...very important that we maintain the link to that spring. It's our village's only fresh water supply. You, or one of your group here, have broken the union three times. Why did you do that?"

Rachel considered her response carefully, while at the same time berating herself for having been stupid enough to divulge the number in her band. She looked around but could not spot the rest of their help. The well-dressed young woman who looked to be about Rachel's own age certainly didn't look like much of a warrior. The other male, even younger than the female, looked to be about as friendly, and perhaps as goofy as they came.

She considered Joe, the one in her band who tried to knife the bull. Silently she cursed the little man's rage. It was Joe's way to attack and ask questions later. This whole mess was his fault, but as usual, she'd have to get them out of it. She'd give him a piece of her mind later and maybe even tell him to get on somewhere else. Take his trouble with him.

"Didn't mean any harm. We were just passin' through, fillin' our jugs. We'll be movin' on now." Rachel waited.

The bull considered her for a moment. "Didn't you read

the sign? I put it here three times personally. It said PLEASE DO NOT TAMPER WITH THIS CONNECTION. PROPERTY OF ROCKTOWN VILLAGERS. It's very well hidden and it is on private property. How did you even find it?"

Before Rachel could form a reply, the bull moved as fast as lightning, notched an arrow and shot it through Joe's hand. He had worked the bands loose somehow and was in the process of throwing a knife at the bull's younger brother. It was a clean shot through Joe's hand, but the arrow was a few seconds short of disarming the throw. The knife had missed it's original target and hit Sarah instead.

Rachel stared in stunned silence for long seconds before she gave a powerful round kick and knocked Joe out cold. Only then did she go to Sarah's still form lying on the ground. The bull was already there, pulling the knife out, trying to stop the bleeding. But Joe's mark had been true. It had only jerked a little to the right when the arrow pierced his hand— where Sarah had been standing beside the other man.

Blood covered the ground by Sarah and the wound looked to be very close to the heart. Just as the panic started to seize her, Rachel reached inside and turned it off. There was no more room to put in hurt and pain, so she just refused it.

"I'll dig the grave over there, right by your precious water union. That okay with you?" Rachel stared with cold, dark eyes at the bull, waiting for his answer.

"Grave? What are you talking about? She's not dead! We've got to get her to the village. NOW!" The last word came with a thundering force when the bull saw the dull, despondent look beginning to overshadow Rachel. He had seen it far too often to miss its meaning.

The bull started barking orders, then looked determined as he asked Rachel, "Can I trust you to free your men and keep them under control while we get your sister the help she needs?"

Rachel nodded. The bull hesitated, searching her eyes, then threw her a knife and started barking orders again.

Within a few minutes they had Sarah pressure-bandaged and on a makeshift stretcher. The bull gave a loud whistle and three horses ran to him from the forest. Within a few more minutes Sarah's stretcher was tied to the bull's horse, the other two were mounted and ready to go, and the bull was holding his hand down to Rachel.

She clasped his hand, leaped up behind him, and was off at a slow trot. He shouted to the other two, "Go on ahead and get things ready."

Rachel looked over her shoulder and shouted to her men, "Follow."

The older bearded man nodded and raised his hand to let her know he understood. Before she turned around she saw Joe trying to raise up and recover from her kick, and as she was losing sight of them saw Troy land Joe with another powerful kick. He raised his hand as before to signal all was well, but this time he added a grin. Only Rachel who knew Troy so well would have seen it through his scraggly beard and rotten black teeth.

Still smiling to herself, Rachel was catapulted back to reality when she started sliding off the horse's rounded rear end. They had started up a steep incline and Rachel had to wrap both arms around the bull to keep from ending up on the stretcher with Sarah.

Sarah. Would Sarah die? Everybody dies. Again Rachel switched it off and just held on.

"Now I'm the one who can't breathe! Ever rode a horse before?" The bull turned slightly in the saddle as he spoke.

"Course I have!" Rachel said as she loosened her hold, suddenly feeling very self-conscious.

Sensing her discomfort, he directed his attention back to managing the horse. His thoughts drifted as he considered the events of the last half-hour that landed that poor girl with a knife so near her heart. She could die so easily, and all he could do was sit atop his horse and guide him one step at a time. There were no rescue helicopters, or ambulances or big sterile hospitals waiting to receive her with teams of doctors standing by. How had the world come to this so quickly?

It had only been a few short years ago since he had cut his leg badly. He could still smell the sterile white and stainless building, see the flashing lights of the ambulance, hear the hum and crackle of all the crisp white medical clothing.

His return to the present alarmed him more than usual. The steady rolling of the dust, ever traveling, carried with it whispers of all the agony and sacrifice, and the constant leaching from the earth, leaving less and less behind for those striving to eat from its broken bounty.

Funny, really. Gone were all the high stress, fast moving days of prosperity. Now the only thing that really mattered was each other—and food, and the one thing capable of producing food refused to work her magic. Mother Earth was turning down all offers—and he couldn't blame her really. She was making a statement that no one could ignore any longer.

All the floods, storms, draughts and erosions finally downed most of the electrical poles, and the glitches, bombs and sabotage crashed or disabled the satellites so many times that they just stopped repairing them. The news had been encouraging before that. It blared from the TV sets around the world telling people to just hold on and not to panic. The polished faces said not to stock up or hoard the food stuffs or it would cause an artificial shortage and inflate prices for everyone. The word was just to have faith in the great scientists of the day and they would heal the parched ground and poisoned water and remove the red haze that prevented the sun from releasing his growing powers and rays of warmth.

When communications started going down, it was alarming how quickly people banded into renegade groups, their one goal to take what they wanted. The public facilities, stores and factories that tried to stay open were repeatedly vandalized and the workers threatened until they either closed or connected with a group for protection in exchange for exclusive buying rights. The results were the same either way—general public deprivation.

In a matter of a few months a whole country had gone from modern, interdependent states back to a pre-industrial era, dotted from coast to coast with villages and groups surviving on whatever they could find to eat and were able to protect from others who would take it.

Over the next few years things had only gotten worse. At first someone could go out under the cover of night and bring back canned goods, animals, and for a while, fruits and vegetables. Most people thought the situation was just temporary, that the government would get the phones, TVs, and computers back up and running. That the military would be dispatched to distribute the government's vast storehouse to the state's citizens.

The bull marveled anew. How could it be that no one really knew the whole story of why that never happened?

He supposed it had a lot to do with the fact that few people dared to travel any distance back then and fewer still lived to tell about it. The occasional traveler would stop in his friendly village and tell his stories. Each one was different from the other and some had obviously been making it up as they went, simply telling a story for a bowl of soup or a cup of water. Some would say that the military was preoccupied protecting the country's borders from conquerors in its weakened state, other's would say the whole world was in the same condition as they were, so the military had simply disbanded, allowing soldiers to care for and protect their own families.

The ground and the water were so poisoned that their attempts to grow food or livestock had been pitiful at best. The shifting soil from the years of flood followed by drought and high winds left the air filled with dust, and the sun and moon weren't functioning properly. One could still feel the urgency of the day. There was nothing to do about it, though, until the time was fulfilled. He could only survive today, one more day—and pray.

His eyes shifted back once again to the girl lying on the stretcher behind his horse. Still no movement. How he wished there was some way to make the trip to the village go faster. He thought of the village's gasoline reserves and stored vehicles that they were still forbidden to use. His eyes met Rachel's and was surprised to find hers looking deeply into his. He found himself lost in their bright blue depths and felt strangely deprived when he turned away.

Rachel shifted uncomfortably behind the saddle. She had to hold on tightly to the big bull or she'd start slipping again. Curse the idiots who first thought of riding such a beast anyway. She was sure she'd never been more uncomfortable in her life. The worst part was holding onto *him*. But in spite of herself she recalled those big honey-brown eyes looking back so sorrowfully at Sarah like he really cared. She'd never seen a man look like that before.

* * * *

Their arrival at Rocktown Village had marked another distressing moment in Rachel's life. It had taken her about five minutes to see how completely out of place she and her band would be there. From outside the high boundary wall that surrounded the village it had looked as though it might be a safe place to take advantage of their host's guilt and rest a few days. Maybe even get a decent meal or two if they were lucky. But as soon as Rachel entered through their gate and saw the beautiful, well maintained houses and perfectly manicured grounds, she had known she didn't fit.

Now she stared down at Sarah and wondered again how she had gotten roped into hanging around this place for so long. There was nothing she could do for Sarah. She would either live or die, and the living part was looking less likely each day. What she wanted had never made any difference anyway, so why wish either way? Just take what you get and be done with it.

It had been three miserable days since she'd arrived here and Rachel was sure she could not survive another. When she had mentioned leaving yesterday, Michael, the bull, had looked at her as if she had murdered someone. She

8

supposed sitting around this sick room showed some kind of loyalty or something toward Sarah in these villagers' eyes, but it was just a plain waste of time.

Rachel got up and moved toward the door to go outside, to take a walk or something, anything to get out of the silent room. She walked right into Michael coming in the door.

"Oh, sorry. How is Sarah today?" Michael moved quickly away from Rachel and walked over to look down at Sarah.

"Still the same. She just lies there." Rachel watched Michael as he took Sarah's hand gently in his and considered how he treated the rest of her band as though they had the leprosy they had managed to escape. She gave voice to her thoughts, "I'm not a leper, you know. You can see that I don't have it. You'd think somethin' burned you when you touched me a minute ago. There's nothin' I can do to help Sarah. I'm gonna be movin' on now. I'll come back to see if Sarah makes it in a week or two."

Michael just stood there with his jaw open, unable to believe the callused attitude this imitation of a woman had toward her own sister. All of the pent up guilt over Sarah and the stress of having her filthy and vulgar band inside their walls for three days finally gave way.

"Rachel, I think that might be just the thing to do. Then the young people in my village will not have to listen to the vulgarity of those...those men out there, and I do use the term men loosely in this instance. And I won't have to come in here several times a day and become disgusted that Sarah's own sister doesn't care whether she lives or dies, and I won't have to smell you when I walk in here! Do you ever take a bath?" Michael sat down in an exhausted slump in the chair near Sarah's bed which had been put there for Rachel's use, though she had never sat in it.

Rachel watched something that looked like shame flood over Michael in the next minute, but was still unable to control the unusual wave of embarrassment the truth of his words brought. When she tried to muster up what would have been her normal response to such a challenge, probably a chair over his head with a few choice words, she could do nothing but shrug her exhausted deference. "No one offered a bath. This is your village, you're in charge, why don't you shut their mouths for 'em? And I would do whatever your doctor asked me to do for Sarah, but there is nothin'. So I will be goin' to find somethin' to eat now. I'll be back in a week or so."

Again Michael was caught with an open jaw. He watched the stringy-haired blond wisp of a girl who smelled very badly grab her dirty pack, sling it over her shoulder and head for the door. "Wait. Wait, I'm sorry, I'm just not myself lately. What do you mean you're going to get some food? Isn't ours satisfactory?"

"I wouldn't know, I ain't had any." Rachel simply shrugged again and was out the door and gone before Michael could speak.

Michael watched the very thin woman walk past the four men camped outside the tiny hospital. He watched them throw exasperated gestures her way, then quickly throw their things in their sacks and follow her. Rachel hadn't uttered a word and yet the four roughnecks moved so swiftly to do her bidding. What did she mean she hadn't had any food? His mother had complained that her band had already eaten enough for a small army and had not once said thank you. He watched Rachel disappear through the village gate with a strange mixture of relief and sadness. He wondered if he'd ever see any of them again. Long strides carried Michael swiftly back to his house. He entered through the back door into the kitchen where his mother stood over the stove flipping pancakes. "Mama, do you think we should just bring Sarah over here now? Her sister just left her."

"What? For pity sake! That poor child. It really makes you wonder what some people are made of. Bring her over here and put her in Ben's room. Ben can share with you until she's well." A sudden look of deep concern came over her normally pleasant, happy face. "She is going to get well, isn't

10

she, Michael?"

"I don't know, Mama. She just lies there like she's in peace and doesn't want to move or think...or live."

Margaret Elizabeth Rock, called Maggie, but known to most as just plain Mama, moved swiftly to put her warm, loving arms around her very tall, handsome son. She could not put into words how proud she was of her second-born son. Michael was just a good person, strong and gentle. And caring. She had never seen him as distressed as he had been over this girl. "Oh, honey, she'll be okay. I didn't mean to worry you. She just needs to get her strength back. She was just so skinny and weak to start with, I think. Her heartbeat is strong and she didn't get a fever." She squeezed his hand one more time and finished, "She'll be okay. Go ask Ben to help you and bring her on over here. The company will probably do her good now, help her to wake up."

"I hope you're right. And...Mama, did the sister, Rachel, get food every day?"

"Well, I suppose so. I sent enough out to those...those people traveling with her to feed a whole town! I asked Naomi to keep a check on her and her needs and she said she would. I didn't see her come out of the hospital once, though. Why do you ask?"

"Oh, nothing. Just curious. Where is my little sister?" Michael stuffed a pancake in his mouth and laughed when Mama smacked his hand with the spatula.

"She's not so little anymore and do you even have to ask? She's next door with Christina making more wedding plans." Mama shook her head, but had an indulgent smile on her face.

"Before breakfast?" Michael mumbled through the cake in his mouth, and then joined in a chuckle with Mama. "Poor Peter doesn't realize what he's gotten himself into with that one! What's the date *this* week?"

"Oh, you men! Your father just asked me that a few minutes ago. The date is set, it has been for a month now. It's October 6th. Peter will be home in September. We figured that was long enough to make them wait." Mama's big chocolate-brown eyes sparkled. "It's so romantic!"

Michael scoffed, "What's so romantic about it? They've been in love since fourth grade. I just wish they'd get it done so I don't have to listen to Naomi's romantic ravings any longer."

Mama studied Michael for a minute and stated, "I think I detect a little jealousy in that attitude."

"Maybe so. I'm sorry, I'm just tired." Michael thought about how often he had had to say he was sorry lately. He needed to get a handle on his mouth. He gave Mama a loud smack of a kiss on her cheek and said, "I'm going next door for a minute, I'll be back for a decent portion of those hot cakes, maybe like four or five of them. Will you smack me again?" He dodged her raised spatula and ran out the door.

"What you smacking him for this time?" The tall athletic older man, with the same dark hair as Michael, put an arm around the much shorter, tawny blonde Mama and kissed her full on the lips with a little more passion than usual.

"Well. Aren't we feisty this morning?" Mama smiled into her husband's eyes for a moment, then waved the spatula in the air and said, "That son of yours grabbed a hot cake and stuck the whole thing in his mouth!"

"Ah, that's my boy!" Herbert stretched his long arms high above his dark hair which had bright silver threads around the temples and yawned loudly. He eyed his wife of thirty-one years. "Something bothering you?"

"You know me too well, don't you? That young woman left a few minutes ago, and thank goodness she took those foul men with her. Now we have to bring Sarah over here to watch after her since her sister deserted her."

"That's what's bothering you? You should be happy they're gone. And you usually jump at the chance to use your nursing skills, so what's really bothering you?" Herbert, most affectionately known as Pops, stood very still and tried hard to curb his natural inclination to make a joke to rid the air of the tension. He had learned over the years that women just need someone to listen to them sometimes, and they don't appreciate humor when they need an ear.

"I know this sounds ridiculous, but I think Michael was attracted to that young woman. Rachel, that was her name, right? Anyway, I've never seen him so upset and irritable."

Pops tried hard to recall the young woman. All he could remember was a thin, wisp of a girl with scraggly blonde hair who wore men's clothing and looked like she needed a bath. He thought of Michael and the beautiful young women, especially the more reserved, intelligent ones that he spent most of his time with, and just shook his head.

"Maggie, I respect your woman's intuition, and goodness knows you're right most of the time, but I think you've mistaken Michael's compassion toward her for having had part in her sister's injury as an attraction. He just feels guilty." Pops thought again of his handsome, sophisticated, always-the-leader, can-have-any-woman-he-wants Michael with the wispy drifting tomboy who smells bad and added, "I don't think you'll have to worry about a wedding invitation with their names on it." Pops chuckled in spite of himself.

"This is one time I hope I'm wrong." Mama wasn't at all convinced, but decided to let the subject drop.

Michael walked in the back door of the house next door and into a kitchen identical to his, at least in the way it was built. They were the only two houses with the same floor plan in the whole village and it was greatly appreciated by the family that they had been able to purchase homes so close together.

The hum of activity inside quickly revealed that the construction was the only thing they had in common. Michael had barely walked through the door when two red-haired children screamed, "Uncle Michael" and ran into his waiting arms. The six-year old identical twins wrapped their arms around Michael's neck and their bright green eyes shone with the love they had for their uncle.

"How's my munchkins today?" Michael "wooled" both

their heads and set them down on the floor just in time to catch the body of three-year old Jeremy as he catapulted into his chest.

"Whoa, you little beast!" Michael lifted Jeremy up over his head and shook him good, then set him on the floor with a firm pat on his bottom.

"I ain't no beast," Jeremy shouted as he took off after his next round of adventure.

"Yuck!" Michael bellowed as he looked down and saw squishy, brown stuff all over his shirt and falling out of his hair.

Christina hurried over with baby Jeremiah in her arms and started wiping Michael's shirt with a wet cloth. "I'm sorry Michael. But you should never let Jeremy touch you! He's always into some kind of foul concoction."

"If this is the kind of treatment I get, I might pick Jeremy up more often." Michael smiled down at his beautiful fiery-haired sister-in-law, "Good morning, Christina. It's okay. Would you stop!"

Michael's older brother, Adam, walked into the room and over to his wife and dropped a possessive arm around her shoulders, "Go find your own woman. This one is most definitely mine."

"Well, big brother, it is very unlikely I'll find one as good as yours, but I plan to keep looking." Michael grinned and winked at Christina and slapped his brother—who was just as tall as he was—on the back.

Adam held both arms out to baby Jeremiah, but as usual he grabbed on tighter to his mother and continued with his whining. Christina gave her husband a thank-you-anyway look and hurried back to the stove where Cream of Wheat was simmering and biscuits were baking.

Naomi came bursting into the room holding a piece of fabric in front of her, "Oh look, Christina, I found this piece of material that will make a beautiful cover for the reception table!" She playfully tapped Michael on the back of the head as she went by, since she was only two inches shorter than her big brothers.

Christina examined the fabric while alernating holding baby Jeremiah, stirring the wheat and taking the biscuits out of the oven. "You're right, Naomi. It's perfect. It's yours."

Naomi smiled at her sister-in-law, gave her a kiss on the cheek and said, "Thank you. See you later today." She headed for the door.

Michael said, "Hey, wait a sec, Naomi." Looking over his shoulder, he called to Adam, "See you guys later." He caught up with Naomi just outside the door and they began walking back to their house.

"How have your visits with Rachel been going? Did she need anything?"

"Rachel who?" Naomi asked innocently.

"The woman with the sister we almost killed, you nitwit." Michael found himself surprisingly impatient with his sister and the verbal sparring he usually enjoyed.

"Hey, don't get huffy with me, and we didn't almost kill anyone. If you'll recall, one of their men threw the knife, not one of ours. But to answer your question, you know I've been busy. I did, however, go by the hospital yesterday and found Rachel sleeping. I didn't want to bother her. I'll go over after breakfast. Okay?"

For the third time today, before breakfast, Michael stood open-jawed, speechless, over a wiry little blonde wisp that he'd probably never see again. But if he did see her again, it seemed he owed her a big apology.

Dark Rain

Chapter 2
One Month Later

The day had been a particularly miserable one. Rachel pulled the old piece of plastic more securely over her head. Shivers ran the length of her body from the sudden drop in temperature. It had been 115 degrees an hour ago, now it hovered around 40 degrees and drizzled something from the April sky that burned any exposed skin. The time of day was indiscernible, everywhere it was a deep dense gray that collapsed inward.

"Come on, Rach, let's find someplace for the night. We'll just get lost in this and it's gettin' late anyhow." Troy shook his head and the foul moisture that was beaded on his long beard and hair dropped to the ground.

"Don't that stuff burn you, Troy?" Rachel stared out from under the plastic, being careful not to let the drizzle touch her skin.

"Naw. Is over there okay?" Troy pointed toward a big oak tree.

"It'll do." Rachel was satisfied with Troy's camp location for the night, but she wasn't satisfied with his answer about the drizzle. "If this stuff don't burn you, then you're brain dead—you know, no more signals. That it?" Rachel grinned.

Troy ignored her barb, glad she hadn't figured out how true her statement was. He looked behind him where the other three band members drudged along and motioned toward the tree. William, the tallest one of the three motioned that he understood. The whistles and cheers from the other two let Troy and Rachel know they approved of the change in plans.

They'd been pushing hard since dawn in the direction of that prissy little village and they'd all made their feelings perfectly clear on how they felt about going back there. Then Rachel reminded them of the food that would probably be available. They'd backed off a little, but not before Joe had spouted out Rachel's deepest fear of the last month: "That scrawny little witch ain't there anyhow, she's done dried up weeks back. What we gotta go all that way back for?"

Rachel had looked away quickly before any of them could see the fear in her eyes that it might be true, or the hate she was developing for the little imp of a man who had knifed Sarah, accident or not. But as it turned out, her younger brother, Daniel, had diffused the situation by picking up a handful of bat dung, sprinkling it over Joe's head and saying, "Here's what we all think of your opinion. Sides, nobody's draggin' you anywhere. Leave if you want to."

Daniel was only sixteen years old and incredibly lanky, but he towered over Joe in height and had developed enough fighting skills over the years to give most full-grown men some grief. Rachel had purposely let him take a lot of grief himself so he'd be strong and able to take care of himself if something happened to her. He'd always disliked her for that, and his challenges toward her had become more intense during the last year. He hadn't stepped in out of loyalty to either of his sisters, he had none. He just enjoyed giving Joe a hard time, and for once Rachel had been glad he did.

Troy brought Rachel back to the present when he became still and raised one arm, a signal they all understood well. He pointed two fingers in one direction and then two in the opposite direction. William and Daniel went one way while Rachel and Joe went the other. Troy walked in a few more yards and tossed out toward the tree, "Evening. Mind if I join you?"

"I...I guess that be okay," came the feminine reply.

Troy moved in and saw a teenage girl and what looked to be an elderly woman lying next to her. "You women alone?"

"Are you?" came the frightened reply.

"Naw, I'm not alone, but we won't hurt you none. We could build you and your friend there a fire if'n you'd be willin' to share the shelter of this ole tree." Troy waited.

"Okay. But I warn you, I have gun," blurted the girl with the strange accent as she scooted closer to the old woman.

Troy just nodded and motioned for William and Daniel to come in. They had a fire going within a few minutes, but Troy still waited another ten minutes before he was satisfied that it was safe to motion Rachel in. Joe came in sputtering about being left out in the wet so long, but Rachel just went over to the fire and warmed her hands, appreciative of Troy's caution.

Troy added some downed tree limbs to the fire and illumination dispelled some of the darkness from under the tree. The tiny gasp slipped from Rachel before she could squelch it. The old woman lying by the girl had large, open sores all over her face and from the severity of the deformity and the smell, they'd been there for quite some time. When the girl put her head to her knees and started weeping softly, William walked over and stood awkwardly for a minute before asking, "What's ailin' you?"

William was six feet four inches tall, weighed about three-hundred pounds, had a dirty-brown, slightly balding mop of hair with large faded-green eyes and a mean temper if you got him riled up. But for the most part, William was a puppy. He just stood there patiently waiting for the girl to acknowledge him. He flashed a warning glare at Daniel and Joe when they started grinning.

The young woman finally realized the big burly guy wasn't going away, so she looked up through her tears. She was surprised to see someone who seemed to notice that she was alive, seemed to notice that she was in an agony so deep that death would be a reward. She had watched everyone in her family, everyone she loved, die, one at a time, a horrible, painful death. The plagues that had killed millions had subsided a few years ago. They thought they had made it on their own, and were proud they had never joined one of the Christian villages with their strange customs. Now she was going to die next, and no one cared. There was no one left to care. Granny would soon be gone. She didn't recognize anyone anymore, her mind chewed to shreds by the disease and the constant pain. Granny had been the strong, positive one. She'd promised that it wouldn't get her, that she'd always be there to take care of her family.

She didn't know what to do, where to go. She'd run from their little shack in a panic to find someone to help. But there had been no one, and she couldn't carry Granny any further. She felt exhausted to the bone and hadn't eaten in two days. She was so cold.

Rachel watched the fear play across the young woman's face. Then came the despair she herself knew so well. Rachel wanted to scream at her to get up, to not give up. To fight.

She didn't have to. As if on cue the girl jumped up, ran straight into William and began beating him in the chest with both fists, screaming and yelling until the night echoed her agony. William stood there, deflecting an occasional wild blow toward his face, but letting her give action to the demon she fought.

When she was spent and slumped into him, William picked her up and held her like a baby. She looked so small and helpless in his huge, beefy arms. They sat by the fire like that for a long time, no one speaking, everyone recognizing her pain.

Joe showed back up with an opossum and a rabbit. No one was surprised that he'd left without saying a word or that he had come back with food. He threw the animals down near the fire along with a few potatoes that had long since seen better days and simply sat down and joined in the melancholy.

It was Daniel who finally broke the trance by picking up the animals, walking a few feet away, pulling a knife from its sheath and began cleaning their supper. It was after the smell of the meat wafted over to her that the young woman finally stirred in William's cradle. She looked around in shame, her eyes going quickly to the old woman lying alone by the tree. She pushed herself from William's reluctant release and quickly shuffled over to the old woman, rubbing her arms from the chill that assaulted her upon leaving her cocoon.

Moments later she fell to the ground and wept, a bitter, mournful cry. She was still there, crouched by the body when Troy walked over to Rachel, spread out the plastic, then the blanket and waited for Rachel to join him. Rachel gave a small sigh, but resigned herself again to the role she played and walked over and took her position next to the bearded older man. As she drifted into a restless sleep, wondering what her visit to the village tomorrow would bring, she felt Troy drape a familiar arm around her waist.

Much later, Rachel felt more than she heard the particular action that only a shovel can perform as it pierces the earth. It carried with it a tearing asunder grind and groan that testified of the grief it buried. Somewhere in her stupor Rachel realized it was William manning the shovel and he who stood and watched the young woman walk away a little before dawn. Rachel's demons held her captive a little longer than usual that grim night.

* * * *

The knock was barely heard above the laughter in the room. Ben heard it since he was listening for one of his friends to stop by—a female friend. He walked away from the door with something quite different than the hello kiss he had wanted. He hurried over to Michael who was listening attentively to Sarah's latest tale. The room burst into laughter again at something she said just as Ben approached Michael.

"She's back, Michael." Ben looked at Michael's puzzled expression and said again, "She's back. Rachel's back. She's right outside the gate."

Sarah heard Ben the second time and got up slowly. Without a word she headed toward the door. Her expression was unreadable, numb. Everyone in the room fell silent, even the children.

"Wait a minute, Sarah. I'll go with you," Ben offered.

She surprised everyone, including Ben, by taking his hand and accepting his offer. Michael got up and followed.

Rachel was the only one standing there when they opened the village gate. She was still dressed in the same men's clothing, but she looked as though she had just had a bath and her hair was brushed. She had that shiny complexion that's only present on your face right after a good scrubbing. She looked quickly at Michael, then at Sarah and Ben's linked hands before looking directly at Sarah and saying, "So you made it okay, huh?"

"Yeah. I made it." Sarah slipped back into the timid creature she had been that first week or two. She lowered her head and looked at the ground as she waited for Rachel to make the next move.

"So you ready to go or what?" Rachel asked.

Ben gave Sarah's hand a firm squeeze, strong emotions filling him at the prospect of Sarah's leaving. As casually as he could manage, Ben said, "It's late. Why don't the both of you come in for something to drink and we'll catch up on the news." He smiled at Rachel and looked to Michael for confirmation.

"Well, it sounds like a plan to me. How are you, Rachel?" Michael asked.

"Fine. Glad it finally stopped the drizzle. The stuff's like acid on your skin." Rachel shifted nervously.

Michael looked at Rachel and decided she'd gained a little weight. The speech he'd rehearsed in his mind so many times just evaporated as he looked into the still blue of her eyes. He blurted, "Are you hungry? I think I owe you a few meals...and an apology."

"You don't owe me nothin'," Rachel stated. "If there's any owin' to be done, I guess it's me who owes you for takin' care of her."

It was obvious to Michael that Rachel was taking her

debt seriously. Michael was known for his compassion, but would not demonstrate it today. He glanced at Sarah and saw the regret and disgrace she felt and it gave him the push he needed. Uncommon anger flashed in his soft brown eyes. "It took long enough for you to realize your obligations. What if things had been different, what if Sarah...." Michael glanced toward Sarah and saw the tears brimming in her eyes and looked back at Rachel with renewed anger.

"I would pay up either way," Rachel stated.

The tired, defeated look that came into her eyes appeased Michael somewhat. He turned around, walked a few steps off and tried to compose himself.

In spite of the stress that was almost tangible, Ben managed to be himself. "Well, Rachel, it looks like my big, strong brother is having a hard time deciding what to do with you, so how about a steaming cup of herb tea until he figures out how to make you pay?" The reckless grin Ben flashed at Rachel lightened her mood.

Rachel decided to join forces with Ben. "Have you got any of those cakes that your Mama kept sendin' out to the men while we was here before? I wanted one for three days." Satisfied with the contrite look she received from Michael, she took Ben's other hand and let him lead her toward their house. When the realization struck that she was holding hands with the man who had part in capturing her whole band just a few weeks before, Rachel shook her head and thought what strange things she had herself doing around these people.

Sarah was having a hard time with Rachel's behavior, too. She kept peeking over Ben's shoulder snatching looks at Rachel. She couldn't believe her sister had been friendly to Ben, but it was impossible that she was holding his hand. Maybe Rachel was ill.

Sarah asked timidly, "Rachel, are...are you sick or somethin'?"

"Yeah, Sarah, I am, and I might as well enjoy every minute of it." Rachel smiled with satisfaction when everyone stared at her.

They reached the house and heard the commotion from the yard. Rachel stood back and watched the frantic crowd, listening until she untangled the mystery. It seemed that Michael's big brother, Adam, had a kid missing. It didn't surprise her. She'd watched the two houses that held Michael's clan for three days from the hospital window and it was a crazy bunch. Kids running everywhere, people always rushing in and out. It took her a while to figure out who lived where and who was married to whom.

Rachel remembered one of the little boys in particular running off constantly and how hard the red-haired woman had tried to keep up with him while wagging her baby around. The older boy and girl that had hair just like their Mama did pretty much whatever they wanted to. They mostly followed Michael around, and he seemed to enjoy it. That had baffled her.

Through her thoughts Rachel heard Sarah's voice, "Rachel can find him." When no one paid any attention to Sarah she said it louder the second time, "Listen to me, Rachel can find him!"

Rachel watched as Michael put an arm around Sarah's shoulders and soothed her as though she were the hysterical one. Sarah was not to be silenced though, her next loud statement brought her more attention, "I love Jeremy too, and I'm tellin' you all that Rachel can find him." Sarah's flood of tears that followed brought Adam and his wife, Christina to her side.

Christina soothed, "Sarah, it's all right, honey. We'll find him, we always have. I'm his mommy, I know." Her bravery faded some as she went on, "I know he's never been gone this long before, but...." Christina burst into tears and Adam ended up holding both his wife and Sarah.

Rachel couldn't believe Sarah was acting like this. She sighed in disgust just as Michael and his mother started staring at her. "What!" Rachel shouted her indignation.

Michael's mother, the one everybody called "Mama,"

pulled Michael along with her and stood very close to Rachel. "Honey, can you find our Jeremy for us? He's so small and helpless. Please, can you help us? He's never been gone this long before. We...we just got busy enjoying ourselves and...." The tears flowed silently down her rosy cheeks.

Sarah had walked over by then and she sobbed, "It's all 'cause I was tellin' stories and none of us was payin' any attention to him.... I'm so sorry!"

Adam and Christina joined in the fray, both saying at the same time, "It's our fault, not yours." Christina sobbed into Adam's shoulder, "It's my fault, I'm the mother!"

Rachel had heard about all she could stand. She stated, "None of that really matters." She directed her attention to Michael and his mother, since they seemed to be somewhat sane. "How long has he been gone?"

Michael sighed and gave one of his tolerant looks toward Rachel, "The twins told us they saw him heading toward the woods right after supper. They told him to go back home and he said he would. He's probably watching and laughing at us right now."

Rachel looked around and knew neither Michael nor anyone else believed that to be true. "So when was supper?" she asked.

Mama stepped in closer to Rachel and answered before Michael had the chance to speak again. She would give him a piece of her mind later for standing there saying something he knew to be false. Everyone felt that Jeremy was in danger, it was thick in the air. "It was a little over two hours ago."

Rachel continued, "Which way was he goin'?"

Adam and Michael stepped forward at the same time, but Michael allowed Adam to speak, "Rachel, we appreciate your concern, but we'll get all the villagers together and go search for him. Please come along and help us if you can."

Sarah rushed forward and shoved both her fists hard into Adam's chest. "Adam! You don't understand. Listen to me! If everybody starts trampin' up all the tracks, Rachel won't be able to find him. Somethin' will kill him before you get to him. Please! Let her go. She can find anythin'. She always could."

Everyone stood in shock for a moment before Michael spoke in his no-nonsense leader's voice, "Listen, Sarah. I know you mean well, but what can one woman do that a bunch of people can't do? The dust line is going to blow away his little tracks anyway...." Too late Michael looked at Christina and saw her panic rising. Michael and Adam each took one of Christina's clammy arms and headed for the house.

Rachel waited until they were out of hearing range, then looked directly to Michael's mother for her answers this time, "Which direction?"

Mama didn't hesitate, "North through the woods over there." She pointed behind their houses toward a dense forest of pine just beyond the village wall.

Rachel moved closer to Sarah and whispered, "The wind won't lift the tracks in those woods for a while. I'll find him." As an afterthought she added, "Troy and the others are just west of the village gate. Go tell 'em to keep these villagers busy in the woods so they won't mess up the trail."

Sarah nodded with enthusiasm and whispered after Rachel, "Thank you, Rach."

Michael and Adam walked back outside just as Rachel was leaving. They looked at each other for a moment and just shrugged as Rachel walked away. Adam stated, "I guess she didn't want to help."

After a moment's indulgence of pure sadness over Rachel's speedy departure from his life again, Michael immediately started barking orders and assembling a search party.

The long hours of the night went excruciatingly slow for Mama, Christina and the three children. Even the twins sat in a stupor for hours before finally falling asleep. Everyone else, including Naomi, was out looking for little Jeremy.

It wasn't long after dawn when Michael and the others came back plastered with brown dust and stricken expressions as they faced Christina's pale, shattered face. She ran to

Adam and sobbed, "Oh no. God, no."

Michael's father, Pops, went quickly to Mama and held her tight. "Maggie, we did the best we could, honey. We'll go right back out after we eat and change our clothes. I promise." His words did little to curb the racking sobs that followed.

Michael walked over and began talking to Pops. "I just don't get it, Pops. I've never seen the villagers so noisy and clumsy. Bill fell down and broke his leg, and it took four men to carry him out. The Nealson boys ended up in a fight. One said the other one tripped him three times. Naomi said somebody grabbed her, but let go and ran away when Ben came by. Old George swears someone was brushing the tracks away. I guess he felt guilty over not being able to follow Jeremy's trail. And I don't know what happened to Sarah. She was there with us at first, then she disappeared."

"I don't know what was going on, son. I guess everybody's just upset over Jeremy. We'll try again in a few minutes. Let's get something to eat, fill our water jugs and head back out. Okay?" Pops waited for Michael's nod of agreement then gave Mama one last squeeze and shoved her gently toward the kitchen. He knew she'd be calmer if she was doing something to help. Pops called after Maggie, "Have you seen Sarah?"

Mama just shook her head and kept walking into the kitchen.

Thirty minutes later as Pops, Adam, Michael, Ben and Naomi were filing out the door to resume the search, Naomi pointed toward the woods and shouted, "Look! It's Rachel and she's carrying something."

Everyone rushed to her. Michael got there first and saw the bloody bundle in her arms. His eyes searched Rachel's and immediately found comfort there. "He's okay, then?"

Rachel nodded. She tried to continue to walk, but blessed blackness set in, the pain finally leaving. Michael caught her and Jeremy before they hit the ground and it was then that he noticed Rachel's leg was also soaked in blood and had a tourniquet tied just below the knee.

Sarah had been keeping watch all night, so she met Michael and the others just as they cleared the woods. Michael would consider later how calm she was compared to her hysterics the night before. Sarah asked Michael, "They're okay, ain't they?"

Michael nodded, "I think so. They've been injured and lost some blood, though." He looked around until he made eye contact with Ben. "Go get the doctor." Ben spun around and took off at a full lope for the house next to the hospital where the old doctor lived.

Christina came running from the house and reached for Jeremy, then drew back in fear as she saw the blood-soaked blanket. With Michael's look of encouragement she reached out again to take the still bundle from Rachel's arms. Rachel's eyes flew open as she tightened her grip on the precious package she had protected with her life. Then she thought she was dreaming as she heard the bull's voice next to her ear, "It's okay, Rachel. You made it. You're home. Let Christina have Jeremy so we can take care of him. If you cooperate, I won't have to tie you up."

Rachel managed a slight smile and released her grip on Jeremy. Right before fading out again, she whispered, "A wolverine had him. Was going too fast. Couldn't catch him."

Michael paled. "How...how did you get him back?"

"Had to offer him a better catch." Rachel looked up at Michael and he saw the fear there in her eyes.

"What?" Michael asked, already knowing the answer.

Rachel was silent a moment longer, then said, "Loosen the tourniquet, okay?"

Rachel's last thoughts before slipping into the blackness were of honey-brown eyes filled with concern for her. Maybe. Then the whisper came in confirmation, "I promise I will take care of you this time. Thank you, Rachel. Thank you for Jeremy."

She never remembered being quite so comfortable. Rachel didn't want to open her eyes because she was sure it would end and she'd never feel it again. So soft—and clean smelling. She snuggled deeper into the feathery softness.

The first thing she saw when her eyes flew open was the whiteness. The curtains were white, the big plush covering on top of her was white. The sheets, the rugs, the chair cushions, everything—white. Rachel angrily threw the covering back and moved to get out of the monstrous bed, but the pain that seared through her leg made her collapse back into its softness.

"Well, my goodness, young lady. You're awake!" Mama hurried into the room and started covering Rachel with the goose-down comforter. "Now, don't you even consider moving that leg. It has seventy-three stitches in it!"

Rachel started to speak when the busy little woman shoved a straw to her lips. Rachel was so thirsty her mouth eagerly drank with a will all its own. Normally she wouldn't have considered drinking anything without treating it first. After a few large gulps, the smell and taste of the liquid hit her senses and she spewed the foul stuff from her mouth and sputtered, "What is this?"

Mama looked at the ugly orange-brown stains all over her favorite guest comforter and tried to shrug it away, "It's an herb mixture that will help you get back on your feet. Now, let's get this cleaned up and get you something to eat. You've been asleep all day. You must be starving!"

The hurt that passed across the older woman's face because of the mess on her precious cover just fueled Rachel's anger at waking up in a place that made her feel like a dirty pincushion. She snarled, "There ain't nothin' wrong with my feet and I'll be gettin' back on 'em right now." Too many years of hunger and knowing her band's expectations tempered her next statement. She had started to say she didn't need anything from them, but said instead, "Just send the food outside the gate. I'll have one of my men waitin' for it."

The pain she encountered when she stood up was excruciating, but Rachel didn't stop until she reached the front porch steps. The woman was sputtering after her mumbling something about wanting to take care of her until she was well and owing her for saving Jeremy.

Rachel turned and glared at the woman who represented everything she'd never have, "Look, old woman, you don't owe me anything! All I want is to get out of here. Where is Sarah?"

Sarah appeared at her side looking like she had just awakened. "I'm right here, Rachel, you shouldn't...."

One scowl from Rachel stopped Sarah in the middle of her sentence. Rachel bit out, "Help me down off this porch and tell these people good-bye. You won't be comin' back!"

Sarah's eyes immediately filled with tears, "But, Rachel, I don't...."

This time Rachel silenced Sarah by grabbing her arm and giving her a hard jerk, "Just shut up, Sarah, and help me down these steps."

Sarah kept looking back at Mama as she helped Rachel down the steps and toward the gate. Mama's big brown eyes brimmed with tears as she threw Sarah a kiss and held out her hand in a sad farewell gesture.

Rachel was in so much pain that she could not give Sarah the jerk she deserved. What was wrong with her sister? Had she gone stupid around these people, acting like she belonged here or something? Rachel could understand why Sarah had wanted her to get the kid back. Sarah had gotten lost when she was only eleven years old, right after their parents died. It had taken Rachel two days and two nights to find her. That was the reason Rachel had taken a special interest in tracking and swore she'd never let that happen to any kid again. It had taken over a hundred stitches to mend the wounds the bear had left on Sarah.

Shivers still spiraled up her spine as she recalled the small, bloody Sarah wedged between two boulders, back in the crack just far enough to save herself, but not far enough to prevent deep claw strikes on her knees and arms. The vultures had already started circling, but the bear had long since given up and moved on.

The animals were as hungry and vicious as the humans on this depleted planet, the few that were left, and it was just going to get worse. Rachel remembered the torn, jagged wounds the wolverine had left on the little boy's back and asked Sarah, "How bad was the boy?"

Sarah sniffled, which brought an exasperated look from Rachel, and answered, "One hundred and two stitches on his back. But the wounds ain't deep. It was like that beast was carryin' its baby. It was mostly his skin that was torn." Sarah shivered, but Rachel didn't begrudge her that response, knowing she was remembering, too.

Rachel rubbed her sore throat, recalling how many times she had screamed at the boy to be still and not fight or the animal would stop and kill him. She remembered her last desperate attempts to make the animal stop. She had seen her chance when the animal opted to go around a steep ridge with his heavy catch. She had run up that ridge with all the might she had left, reached the trail on the other side before the beast got there, sliced her leg so the blood smell would lure the animal over and just laid there, waiting.

She was sure that had been the longest moment of her life, knowing how fast and ferocious the animal was. She didn't know what scared her the most; that the animal would take her bait or that he'd just keep going with the boy. The wolverine had crept up and clamped his steel-like jaws around her bloody leg before she could raise her knife to stop him. Where her knife ended up had been both a streak of good luck and bad. The blade between the eyes had stopped his aggression almost immediately, but it had also locked his jaw firmly in place. She had created half the injuries to herself getting his sharp teeth out of her flesh.

The remembering seemed to increase the pain in her leg tenfold. Rachel tried to concentrate on something else, but she was already lost to it when Michael came running toward her and Sarah as they approached the gate. It made her so angry that she was too weak to tell him what she thought of him and his people's pushy ways. She wanted to kick him when he told her she wasn't going anywhere until she was stronger. She would just show him how strong she was, and to her mortification, she did. She passed out right into his arms, for the second time in the same pitiful day.

Fading Light

And again, verily I say unto you, the coming of the Lord draweth nigh, and it overtaketh the world as a thief in the night—

Therefore, gird up your loins, that you may be the children of light, and that day shall not overtake you as a thief.

Joseph Smith, 1834

Chapter 3

"Let's go in and get her out," Joe demanded. Troy and Daniel sat by the fire paying little attention to him. "It'll get me my chance to get my hands on that fancy, tall female. I had hold of her in the woods last night, was goin' to get me a real kiss, but that big ox of a brother came along. I'll get her, though." Joe's dark weaselly eyes lit up and the foul gestures that followed irked even his present company.

"So why didn't you give him what for, Joe, and just take what you wanted? Was he just a bit too much of a man for you, or was it the woman who was too much?" Daniel laughed and waited to see if Joe was in the mood to take the bait tonight. Goodness knows Joe had been there to harass Daniel ever since he was a little boy. Well, he wasn't little anymore.

The soft, clear bird call from William who was patrolling the first watch drew all three's attention to the small figure approaching camp. Sarah called, "It's just me, ya'll."

Joe smirked, "Well, well. Looky here whose come to grace us with her presence."

Sarah just ignored the little man's badgering as she had for so many years. She glanced at Troy and he gave her a nod of recognition, then at Daniel who promptly elaborated Joe's sentiments, "Well, hell, Sis. Thought you'd done found yourself somewheres else to be a bother. Guess we ain't that lucky, though."

Sarah was surprised at how angry their words made her. These men hadn't seen her for weeks; hadn't known whether she was dead or alive until last night and it was obvious they didn't care either way. Scenes from the family she'd just left flashed through her mind. She marveled anew at how often they embraced each other, how often they told each other of their love. How often they showed it. Sarah was drawn back to the moment by Joe's beady little eyes and some foul comment about Naomi, Michael and Ben's sister who had helped nurse Sarah back to health for weeks.

"You touch her, you rotten little weasel, and her family'll put your ugly head on a pike!" Sarah breathed heavily, drew herself up and took advantage of Joe's moment of shock by hurrying over to Troy where she felt safer.

Daniel burst out laughing and fanned the fire that burned in Joe's black heart to a new level. Outwardly, Joe just shrugged and tried to act as though Sarah's comments weren't important, but Troy hadn't missed the flash of hatred in the little man's eyes before he masked his emotions.

Troy asked Sarah, "Does Rachel need us to come fetch her?"

Sarah just stood speechless for a minute. Sure, she had spoken to Troy last night, carrying Rachel's orders to detain the villagers in the woods, but that didn't count, really. She couldn't believe he didn't even have a "hello," a "how have you been" or "glad you didn't die"—nothing. It shouldn't have surprised her.

Troy was tolerable enough, maybe he even liked her a little, but he was definitely a loner. He just didn't seem to need anyone but himself—and maybe Rachel. She guessed that was because Rachel had saved him from that snake pit and he felt like he owed her something.

As Sarah looked down at him she saw nothing in the older man's shaggy gray, dirty hair, long beard, rotten-black teeth or very slim build that could possibly interest a young woman like Rachel. A long stream of murky brown tobacco juice spewed from Troy's mouth and added to Sarah's feelings of revulsion. When she calculated in the fact that he openly bragged about his conquest of Rachel, she was convinced there had to be more than she understood since it was so unlike Rachel to ignore such patronizing.

Troy's "Well, do we?" made Sarah realize she hadn't answered his question about whether they needed to fetch Rachel or not.

"No, Troy, she's pretty stove up. Got seventy-three stitches in her leg from that wolverine 'cause she was tryin' to take the boy from him. They're takin' good care of her. She ain't none too happy 'bout it, but she needs it." Sarah thought she saw a thread of compassion streak through Troy's eyes for the boy. Or maybe for Rachel. Or maybe even for her, remembering her close call with the bear and the horrible memories the whole episode brought back to her. Sarah's nightmares had started up again.

"We'll wait here then. Did you bring us some food?" Troy just kept chewing his tobacco, never even looking up at Sarah.

Sarah was sure it had just been her imagination about his compassion. Wishful thinking. She sighed and said, "Yeah. I set the sack over there."

"You be bringin' it tomorrow, too, then?"

"Yeah. See ya'll."

Sarah walked away with an emptiness that made her ache inside. Rachel hated Michael and his family, so she'd make them leave real soon and it would be like it used to be. The tears rolled down her cheeks and landed in the rolling dust near her knees. How could she bear to give up what she'd found? Give up Mama and Pops. Michael and Naomi. Adam, Christina and the four rowdy munchkins. And Ben.

He seemed to materialize from her thoughts. "Sarah, what the heck are you doing out here by yourself?" demanded Ben. He took Sarah by the arm and started dragging her toward the gate as though she were a naughty child.

Sarah sputtered her disgruntlement over his fatherly manner, "Ben, I've lived with the meanest men alive for almost eighteen years. How can there be anything worse than them after me?" She jerked her arm from his hold and surprised herself again by her bravery. She guessed Naomi was rubbing off on her.

Ben had turned red from his anger and demanded, "What! did you just say?"

"I said I've lived with the meanest men alive and I ain't scared anymore!"

"Not that part, the other part." Ben had stopped and turned Sarah toward him and was shaking her. Why had he assumed she was so much younger? Put himself through hell because he thought he was falling for a kid?

"What other part, you idiot. Let me go, you're the one hurtin' me!" Sarah screamed and clutched the area over her heart that was still so tender from the knife wound.

"Oh, Sarah, I'm sorry! Are you all right?" Ben had turned pale with the realization of what he was doing.

"Of course I'm all right. I'm not a baby. Just leave me alone, will you?"

Ben nodded and motioned for Sarah to walk beside him. "Please." They started a slow, silent walk back through the gate of Rocktown Village.

William grinned as he watched Sarah and the young buck. It was about time somebody cared about little Sarah. Out of habit he looked around to give a warning to any who would make fun of him. He grinned again and shook his head when he remembered he was on patrol and no one was there but him. Sometimes he got things mixed up, but he wasn't mixed up about those two, and he wasn't mixed up about his Ginny either. He looked around again for the hundredth time. Excitement coursed through him. It was almost time.

Just a few minutes later he heard the call they'd agreed on using and then the shuffle of her tiny feet. She hurried to him and he held out his arms and gathered her close. For the first time in a long time, William breathed easy again.

Back in the village things were not so good. "Herbert, do you think she has carried something against me with her from another life? She couldn't possibly hate me that badly from anything I've done to her in this life." Mama's large round, honey-brown eyes threatened to spill their pain over at any moment.

This time the occasion deserved some lightening up. Pops was sure of it. "No, Maggie, I don't think it's anything you've done," Pops began quite seriously, "I think it's that little devil riding about in her pocket that made her call me a large maggot an hour ago, and Naomi a pulsating womanly clump earlier today." Pops was mimicking Rachel's odd speech patterns as he spoke. "And don't forget the twins are double turds." Pops held it in for a time until he saw Mama's lips twitching, then roared in laughter.

Pops had to raise an eyebrow at how fast Maggie could still move when she wanted to. Other than a slight bulge around the middle, Maggie still had a fine figure. She had him swatted thoroughly before he knew what hit him. He knew a cover-up when he saw one, though. Pops snatched the dish towel from Mama and proved his suspicion. The minute she was robbed of her camouflage, she burst out laughing with him.

A few minutes later while Mama was still sitting on Pop's lap laughing, Ben strolled by and barked, "I'm sure glad the two of you are enjoying yourselves while the rest of us are being thoroughly abused by that little heathen in my bedroom. I forgot she was in there and walked in to get my jacket and she called me a human jackass! You need to do something about her!"

Pops burst out laughing again and, as ashamed as it made her, Mama joined right in. Ben looked at them both as though they'd lost their minds and stomped toward the door. Mama managed to ask through her giggles, "Where are you going at this hour?"

Ben stood there for a moment shifting an irritated stance back and forth, not knowing where he was going, but knowing he had to get away from those two sisters before he throttled one of them. "Out to eat some grass?"

Ben could still hear his father hooting a block down the street. He was sure his whole household had gone mad, and he was well on his way to joining them.

Rachel slapped Sarah's offer of water away and irately

stated, "I need to get out of here, Sarah. Now are you goin' to help me, or do I have to manage it on my own and slap a knot on you for not mindin' me?"

Sarah looked at Rachel determinedly and shook her head. "You're not goin' anywhere until you're stronger and...and I'm not a baby now, Rachel. I don't think you should be slappin' me anymore."

Rachel was completely taken aback by Sarah's remark. Sarah had never stood up to her before. She wasn't quite sure what to do. She was used to Daniel lipping off at her, and she'd sure given him his fair share of slappings, and in the last year she'd had to use all the skill she could muster to put him on the ground several times until he squealed, "uncle." She wasn't sure how much longer she was going to be able to pull that off. He was getting so strong and agile. She couldn't help but be a little proud of that.

But Sarah. Not Sarah. Quiet, shy, obedient Sarah. Sarah was scared of everything. Wasn't she?

When Rachel just stared at her, not saying anything, Sarah felt compelled to break the silence, "I didn't mean any disrespect, Rach. I'll always try to please you, 'cause...well 'cause you're the only friend I've ever had and...and I know that, but I'm ready to grow up now. Is that okay?"

After a few minutes of continued, awkward silence with Rachel staring at her like she'd seen a ghost, Sarah just walked out of the room and straight into Mama's arms.

"Oh, now honey, it's going to be okay. Rachel's just upset over being cooped up in this house. She'll be all right in a few days." Mama smoothed Sarah's hair and crooned to her in a way only an experienced mother could manage. Mama loved Sarah's hair. It was cropped off right below her ears and was full of naturally sassy, deep chestnut curls. Her apple-green eyes along with the sprinkling of freckles across her nose made her look like a wholesome farm girl off the cover of a magazine. She was so small and frail in Mama's arms, just a child, and look how she had to live. Mama wondered just how old she was.

Now just didn't seem like the right time to ask, she might think she was making fun of her for crying. "Let's go get a cup of hot cocoa. You want to, honey?" Mama continued to hold her and stroke her hair.

Rachel watched with intensity through the crack in the door. She couldn't believe it. That woman was treating Sarah like she was her child. She couldn't hear what they were saying. She didn't have to. She had to get Sarah out of here. She tried to get up again and fell back on the pillow in a gasp of pain. Her leg was getting a fever in it, she could tell. She needed to get it packed in clean mud. Antibiotics were hard to come by and mud was the next best thing. She had to get to her band outside the gate. Troy would help.

Using the nightstand, Rachel gritted her teeth and eased herself over the side of the bed to the floor. When the injured leg touched the floor, black sparkles pulsated in and out across her vision until she was sure she would lose her dinner right there on Ben's bearskin rug. Finally, it passed and Rachel made it to the door just as Naomi knocked lightly.

Rachel saw the tall, female version of the father and oldest brother standing outside the door and cursed her luck again. She peeked through the door with her sickeningly-sweet smile and begged, "Can I come in?"

Rachel growled, "Do I really have a choice?" Rachel looked at her long, silky, very dark hair and her striking shade of gray eyes just like her father's and wanted to slug her. How could her clothes fit her that perfectly? She had on a pink sweater that looked like pearls had been woven into the material. Rachel wanted to touch it to see if it was as soft as it looked. The dark pants were made out of something that shined—silk, she guessed, and they were the perfect length. A fluffy bow tied on top of her head, pink and black, made her look like she was ready to go to a party.

Without a second thought, Naomi took the scarf from around her head and had it tied around Rachel's before Rachel realized what was happening. Naomi had never seen a more longing look than Rachel had just given her clothes, especially the scarf. She took Rachel by the arm and began leading her back to the bed without a word.

This person was crazy, Rachel was sure of it. It was just too stinking bad that she didn't have the strength to do anything but be led by her, back to the bed, with a prissy little bow around her head. She was sure she was going to throw up now, she just hoped she could hold it until this idiot left. Too late.

* * * *

"It's your turn," insisted Ben.

"It definitely is not my turn, I did it last time," countered Naomi.

They both looked at Michael and he raised both hands in the air and stated flatly, "Hey, not me. If you two think she's mean to you, she's completely vicious to me. Called me a polecat one time, and a mule's ass the last time!"

All three burst out laughing, but in the end it was Michael who agreed to go in with the medication. The doctor insisted Rachel take it every four hours to control the infection.

Mama and Pops were enjoying a well-deserved few days away. Pops had inherited a small cabin on twenty acres of land just about five miles out of town. The whole family used to travel there for two weeks every year for summer vacation. It was ironic that they had ended up moving to the area.

The cabin sat upon a hill by a huge oak tree looking out over a beautiful little pond. It was filled with family memories, and a happier time. Mama had longed to go there, to go back, for years. She had asked about the possibility many times.

This had been the first opportunity. It had been planned for weeks and the four kids had to practically push them out the door. A couple of the village's most influential citizens had insisted they needed the time away and that it was safe to travel again. But, nevertheless, they had provided several young men to escort them just in case, so they had no excuses. Pops was the well loved unofficial leader of the village, so his safety and well-being, were taken seriously.

Michael tapped lightly on the door, but didn't expect an answer. He was shocked when he heard Rachel say sweetly, "Please come in."

He looked at her suspiciously and handed her the precious antibiotics that were probably saving her life and a cup of water. Rachel took the pills and handed the cup back to Michael. "Thank you."

Rachel had to smile at the astonished look on Michael's face. "Don't look like I've just asked you to be my bride, Michael. I just decided to try askin' kindly. Would you...please take me out to my camp now. I feel fine and I am goin' to go mad if I have to stay in here another day."

Michael looked down at Rachel's leg that was still swollen to double it's size and still had a nasty red color, then to the sweat that beaded her forehead and knew he couldn't do it. "I wish I could, believe me. But Mama would skin me alive."

"Do you do everythin' your mama tells you to do, Michael? You're a little old to be so close on your mama's skirt-tails," Rachel ended with a irritated smirk.

"I try to," was all Michael said as he headed for the door.

"No, wait! Please, Michael. I can't stand it in this room another minute alone. I'll be nice, I promise. Stay for a while," Rachel begged.

Michael looked at her with renewed suspicion, but walked over and sat in a chair by her bed. It was the close-up view that let Michael see the genuine fear in Rachel's eyes. Maybe the beads of sweat on her forehead weren't from a fever after all. "What's wrong, Rachel?"

"I just don't like bein' alone."

"You have a strange way of showing it," Michael said without any ire.

"I know. Just the way I was raised, I guess."

Michael could see that she was really trying to be civil.

"How were you raised, Rachel?"

As Rachel looked into those caring chocolate-brown eyes, the same ones that Mama had, they compelled her to do something she knew she'd regret later, yet couldn't seem to make herself stop. The last few days had been the worst in her life. Not because she was lame, suffering painfully at times or that she was dependent on these people, rather because they had demonstrated to her over and over again what she had been deprived of her whole life. They had shown her the difference. She hated them for that.

Her ignorance had been bliss compared to the agony she felt now. Hadn't life been rotten enough without adding a new dimension to it?

"That's a long story, Michael. Are you sure you want to hear it?" Rachel waited, knowing how important his answer was, but refusing to admit it.

A simple sure would have gained a sigh of relief from Rachel, because, for the first time in her life, she had to talk to someone. The answer that came was one she would cherish for some time to come.

"Rachel," Michael leaned forward and took her hand in his, "I have never been more positive of anything in my entire life. I will stay and listen until you tell me to leave."

"Why?" was the simple, choked reply from Rachel.

"Because you are important...and I care about you. We all care about you. And one of the reasons why we care, not the only one, mind you, is that you gave Jeremy back to us. Rachel, you can't know how precious he is to us. Unfortunately, people don't realize just how much someone means to them until they're gone. He would be gone if it weren't for your selfless gift. I don't know how we can ever thank you enough. So, I will listen, for as long as you need me to, Rachel."

"I didn't do it for you, I did it for Sarah. So you don't owe me anythin'," Rachel stated.

As Michael saw her slipping back into her cocoon, he said a silent prayer. Please don't let her slip away—help me to know what to say.

"Because Sarah asked you to?" Michael quizzed, hoping it would help to start talking about Sarah, to get Rachel's attention away from herself.

"I guess it's more the reason why she asked me." Rachel went on to tell Michael the whole story about eleven-year-old Sarah and the bear.

Michael had a vivid picture of the timid, little Sarah sandwiched between the crack in the two boulders by the time Rachel finished. It seemed both sisters had a knack for storytelling. But more importantly, Michael had a vision of the frightened young woman who searched for two days and two nights until she found her little sister, bloody and unconscious.

"How old were you Rachel? And where were your parents?" Michael waited to see if Rachel was willing to talk about herself now.

"I was sixteen. Our folks had been killed by robbers just a week before. We were already hid in the woods when it happened, so the robbers didn't see us. They burned our house, so we just left. They was probably mad 'cause they didn't find nothin' to steal." Rachel looked as though she had traveled back in time, and whatever else it had been, it was clear that it had been painful.

"And." At Michael's prompt, Rachel continued, still lost in another time.

"We hated it there, anyhow. I guess Sarah wasn't used to stickin' 'round a campfire, and I wasn't used to keepin' track of an eleven-year-old sister and a ten-year-old brother all the time. They stuck like glue to me the first few days, but when they realized it was safe and nobody was goin' to...hurt them anymore, they got adventurous or somethin'. I've been chasin' 'em ever since." Rachel actually gave a half smile. "Hard to believe that was six years ago."

Michael sat silently contemplating what he had just learned. A little calculating told him Rachel was twenty-two, Sarah seventeen and Daniel sixteen. Goodness, Sarah looked younger than that. Rachel had called them her folks, but nothing in her tone even resembled love or affection for them. She said they were already hid in the woods. Why? She'd said there was nothing there to steal. And what in the world had been hurting Sarah and Daniel before they left, since they felt safe with Rachel later?

Michael asked the safest question he could think of, desperately wanting Rachel to continue talking, "Where was your home that burned?"

"Minnesota." Rachel knew Michael wanted her to talk. She also knew he hadn't missed one of her slips of the tongue. Or were they slips? Maybe she wanted to tell someone, finally. Maybe she was sick of avoiding the subject of her folks and where and how she grew up. Daniel and Sarah never spoke of them, at least not after the first time she threatened to walk off and leave them if they ever mentioned their names in front of her again. Rachel was sorry she'd done that now, but back then it had just hurt too much to let them talk about it. She had hated too deeply.

Rachel knew they all needed to talk about it. How did people begin after all this time to talk about something that was so bad they still had nightmares about it? No one knew their story. Not even the band members. It was all just locked inside the three of them. She knew she was dangerously close to unlocking it when the tears came no matter how hard she tried to stop them.

Michael couldn't let her sit there and bear the pain alone any longer. He got up out of the chair, sat on the edge of the bed and gathered Rachel in his big arms and held her tightly. He told her over and over again that it would be all right, that whatever it was they would work through it together, his family and hers. Michael rubbed her thin shoulders that shook so violently from the sobs that it seemed to rack her soul. He smoothed her hair again and again, soothing her like he had his sister or niece so many times when they were hurt or frightened.

When she had quieted some, Michael whispered, "You

don't need to talk about it until you're ready. I'll be here, I'm not going anywhere."

"I have to. Now. Is that okay?" Rachel pushed him away.

"I'm listening." Michael tried to hide his disgruntlement at how quickly she'd turned cold and pushed him away like a used handkerchief.

"You have to promise me somethin' before I start." Rachel rolled her eyes skyward and mumbled, "I know I'm goin' be sorry for this...."

Michael chose to ignore her mumble and asked, "What?"

"Promise me you'll never tell nobody, and I mean nobody, without me saying so. Agreed?" Rachel held out her hand to make him shake on it.

Michael took the hand of the young woman in front of him who was trying so desperately to turn their budding friendship into a business deal. He brought her hand to his chest and turned her palm until it lay flat across his heart and said, "I promise to take care of, and cherish, everything you share with me."

Rachel stared into the honey-brown of his sincere eyes and began losing her nerve. His long, dark hair had smelled so good and clean, his chest so broad and capable. She had never had anyone hold her and tell her he cared before. Could he be real? Were these people real? No, they couldn't be and she wasn't going to do this stupid thing.

He could feel her slipping away. He did the only thing he could think of, the only thing that came to mind. Michael dropped her hand, got up and headed for the door, tossing over his shoulder, "Just call if you need me, Rachel."

"And never to tell nobody," Rachel demanded.

Michael stopped and turned around, being careful to mask his emotions and holding in the great sigh of relief that welled up within him. "And I promise never to tell anyone."

Rachel nodded and looked down at her hands as Michael came and sat silently in the chair. It was a long time before she spoke again. "I look just like my...my mama. So my daddy didn't like me, he mostly acted like I didn't exist, 'til I hit him one day for...for hurtin' Sarah. He was a mean drunk. I was lucky that he didn't like me." Rachel hugged herself and began moving her hands up and down her arms frantically. She looked at Michael and couldn't continue. How could she put into words what she'd seen him do to her little sister.

Michael thought he knew where the story was going and when he thought of sweet, little Sarah, he wanted to stand up and throw the chair through the wall. But that wasn't what Rachel needed. He had to think of her. He asked very softly, "But your father liked Sarah?"

Rachel nodded, "She looks jus' like him. He used to tell me and Daniel that Sarah was the only one of us that was any 'count 'cause she had his blood. Said the rest of us was worthless, just like our mama and her people." Rachel dropped her head a little more, losing the fight against the words that were still trying to crush her.

"Did Sarah like her father, Rachel?" Michael prompted.

She looked up and shook her head vigorously, "No! We all hated him, all of us! Sarah would cry and look at us for help when he'd pick her up and...and take her away." Rachel looked down and realized she was tearing one of Ben's pillows. She raised her tear stained eyes to Michael's in apology.

Michael put a large, firm hand over both of Rachel's that held the twisted, torn pillow and said, "It's okay. Don't worry about it, it doesn't matter."

"Damn him, Michael, there was times he didn't even close the door!" Rachel screamed, shoving Michael's hand away and tearing at the pillow until the feathers spilled into the air.

Michael wanted to smash something, anything to avenge them their pain. Instead, he stood and took hold of Rachel's wrists so they could control their anger together. She jerked loose and began pounding him in the chest with both fists, still screaming.

Ben, Naomi and Sarah all slammed into the room about

the same time Rachel collapsed against Michael's chest and began sobbing quietly. Michael turned to look at them and motioned for them to leave. They reluctantly filed out of the room, one at a time, until Sarah closed the door behind them.

Rachel sobbed into Michael's chest, "She just watched, Michael. That's all she did. She sat there like a ghost and watched what he did to us. She watched him rape Sarah over and over...and beat Daniel and me when I tried to stop him...then...then he started locking me in the cellar, sometimes for days at a time to get rid of me so I wouldn't try to stop him. It was so awful and dark...and alone down there."

"Who, Rachel, who watched?" Michael asked as he tried to take it all in.

"Mama."

"Oh, God." Michael realized he was holding her so tightly she couldn't possibly be breathing. He released his hold so quickly that Rachel almost fell out of the bed.

The hurt in Rachel's eyes when she looked up at Michael was almost tangible. She shoved him further away and started screaming, "Get out! I don't need you anyway. Get out before you have to touch me again and get your precious hands dirty. Get out!" She started picking up things from the nightstand and throwing them at Michael.

"It's not what you think, Rachel, I...."

"I don't care what you think! Get out! Now!" Rachel picked up Ben's favorite model car that had taken him months to build and glared a warning at Michael.

Michael held both hands in the air and started backing toward the door, "Okay. Okay, I'm leaving, but it's not what you think, I thought I was hurt...."

When Rachel pulled back to throw the car, Michael hurried from the room without ever finishing his sentence. Somehow, Rachel always managed to leave things unfinished with him. He sighed outside the door, then walked down the hall with a heavy heart, mostly because he knew Rachel's was even heavier.

Chapter 4

Mama could not control the steady flow of tears that coursed down her cheeks and fell onto the saddle beneath her. She had seen many who were afflicted with the disease. They had visited their village hospital for treatment in the beginning, but the gate had been closed during the worst years of destruction. Mama had been isolated from it for some time, had believed it was over. Until now. Three days ago the trip to the cabin had been ruined for them after witnessing the horrible condition of the few, but wretched people camped along the road. Pops and Mama had really tried to enjoy their time alone. So many people had worked hard to give them their mini-vacation. After the third day they had decided to stop pretending they weren't lonely and worried about their family and the village. They had looked at each other early on that third morning and said at the same time, "Let's go home."

The young men escorting them had decided to take them across country to escape the newly established encampments along the road since it had upset them so badly on the way there. But there didn't seem to be any escape because the countryside bore its horrors as well, though, thank goodness, a lot less of it. Mama looked over at Pops and saw the pale, drawn look on his handsome face and closed her eyes and sobbed again.

She was drawn from her agony when she felt a tug on her stirrup and looked down into the face of a little girl about Jeremy's age. "Puh-lease, do's you has any food?" One of the young men riding with them quickly ushered her away, but not before Mama had gotten a good look at her face and hands. Mama slapped at the flies swarming around her so violently that she nearly fell off her horse. Pops rode over to her and took hold of her horse's reins, keeping the horses very close together as they rode.

Pops asked, "Are you okay, Maggie?"

Mama just kept staring forward with a look of sheer misery in her glossed-over eyes. "Did you see her little hands, Herbert? Did you see the pain in her eyes? Isn't there something we can do to help them?"

"We've tried. They won't change how they live and join one of the villages. We've all issued invitations and the missionaries keep working among them and treating them, but they just get reinfected with the maggots within a few days at best. It's the conditions they live in, with all those cursed flies. There's not much anyone can do about them. They're here to stay."

Pops looked like he was really dreading the flood of questions that he knew would come from Mama. His worry for her was the true reason for his pallor, not his having experienced the condition of these people. He'd seen it all, time and time again, but had hoped to spare Mama any further exposure to it.

It had been a unanimous vote to build the walls, and then, much later, to close the gate to their village. Each village had established its own set of rules according to the people's wishes and their's had served them well. There was nothing they could do to help the people on the outside, so why subject their little children and women to it?

"Why! Why, Herbert? Why don't we share more with the people outside the gate? We have food, we have some medical supplies. How can we just prosper there within those walls and pretend this doesn't exist out here?"

"Maggie, you know we're not pretending about anything. What do you want to do? Bring that little girl home and put her in bed with Jeremy? Do you want us to open the gate and feed the whole countryside? Our small surpluses would be gone in a week. And they'd plunder and destroy the greenhouses. Then what would we do? The ones that are left are not nice people, Maggie. They've had a hundred opportunities to live differently. They raid and steal and rape."

Pops lowered his voice and reached over and touched Mama's clammy hands that clutched the saddlehorn. "Maggie, we knew this is how it would be if you women knew the extent of it. Don't you see? There's nothing you—or anyone—can do. This is the way it's going to be, for now, anyway."

"Oh, honey, I know. I really do know. I'm sorry I yelled at you. It's just all so sad. The little ones. When will it all end? How long will we live like this, isolated in our own little world?" Mama implored Pops with her eyes to say something to her that would ease the pang in her heart.

"Do you mean the safe, comfortable, peaceful, healthy little village where we are surrounded by so many people that we love? Well, I hope we will have it to be isolated in for as long as it takes, Maggie. For as long as it takes." Pops squeezed her hands one more time then handed her reins back to her and continued riding toward home.

Mama, feeling as though she'd been rightfully chastised, mumbled to herself, "Well. I guess that answered my question."

Pops looked back, "Did you say something?" The look of concern on his sweet face made Mama feel even more guilty.

Mama just shook her head and smiled, a tentative I'm-still-hurting-but-I-understand kind of smile. Pops' face softened and he smiled his own understanding.

The rest of the trip passed in silence. Cold, hard silence. The young men did a good job keeping some distance between them and the scattered campsites. There were still several encounters that would forever haunt Mama's peaceful dreams. One young man had eased himself from his hiding place in a bush and had reached up and grabbed the arm of one of the escorts and demanded that he give them food. When he was told they had none to give, he became angry and spouted vicious accusations, throwing rocks at them as they rode on.

There was no anger in her heart for him, though, because Mama had looked into his eyes, into that hollow place where his soul used to be and had seen his torment. To him, they were on the inside and he was locked on the outside. The thing that really made Mama the saddest was that he was right. It was too late to do anything about it. They had let their opportunities pass them by. For a woman who had believed all her life that it was never too late, that thought really took its toll.

Pops looked over at Mama and apologized again for having brought her out into such a mess. He told her he must have been temporarily insane to have agreed to the trip, but Mama knew the pressure that had been put on him, and now she knew why he had finally given in. She had needed to see this, to understand, so she could help Pops bear the burden that threatened to break even his sturdy back and hardy spirit. She would think it all through and come out stronger as soon as she had some time alone to ponder and pray.

They were only a mile away from the safety of their village gate when the arrows came. One horse was killed, two of the young escorts had arrows in their legs and Mama had one through her right shoulder. Pops grabbed Mama's mount by the reins and raced for the gate after her verbal assurance that she could hold on. Halfway back they heard the bell ringing from the watchtower in the village and met the armed riders that had been sent to help them. Pops had insisted they keep going to help the young men who were still on the road behind them, but they refused to leave their leader until he was safely inside the walls.

Once they were in front of their home, Pops reached up and carefully took Mama into his arms. They were surrounded within seconds by the rest of the family members plus half the village. Nothing like this had happened in a long time, but it brought back horrible memories, so the tension was heavy in the air.

The unshakable, faithful Pops faced his family with huge, worried eyes. Michael immediately tried to take Mama into his younger, stronger arms, but Pops flatly refused.

Adam eyed the arrow that was buried deeply into Mama's shoulder, and asked, "Shouldn't we take her to the hospital, Pops?"

Mama raised her head from its buried position in Pops neck and answered for him in a steady voice, "No, honey, I want to stay at home. Please bring the doctor here."

Ben headed for the hospital before anyone had time to ask him.

Mama's great courage brought tears to several eyes. Pops, Adam and Michael had all lived through arrows in their body and knew the pain she was enduring without a complaint. Pops kneeled beside their bed and eased Mama onto it. He brushed the hair from her forehead and implored, "Will you ever forgive me, Maggie. I'm so sorry. I felt stupid about the trip from the beginning, I should never have taken you outside these walls. I...."

"Herbert, I know exactly why we needed to go. Why you couldn't say no. I understand. Please, just get this thing out of me, okay?" Mama looked down at her blood soaked clothes and the arrow piercing the tender skin near her breast and lost the war against her tears. They flowed steady and true down her pale cheeks.

Adam and Michael reached for Pops at the same time and forced him to sit in the chair near the bed. He had lost all of the color in his face and had begun to sway. Pops looked up at his sons and whispered, "You know what has to be done. Oh, God, we have nothing to stop that kind of pain. Why couldn't it have been me? Not Mama."

The old doctor came rushing in before his sons could respond. The doctor took one look at the arrow and how deeply embedded it was in Mama's shoulder and had to just sit down and look away for a moment. He wasn't a real doctor, just a physician's assistant, and it was times like this that really brought him down; made him feel so inadequate.

Maggie was such a good, sweet woman and the pain she was about to endure just didn't seem fair. If they were lucky she would pass out.

After looking at Pops and receiving a nod of understanding, the doctor looked at Mama and said, "Maggie, we're going to have to push this arrow on through, there's nothing else we can do because of its location and the kind of tip that's on it. Do you understand? It's going to be painful, but it has to be done. And it needs to be done now, so we can stop the bleeding as quickly as possible. Okay?"

All the men looked on with bewildered faces, all wishing it was them instead, and Naomi, Christina, and Sarah sobbed quietly in the background for their beloved, sweet Mama, and what she was about to endure.

Mama reached up with a powerful swipe and ridded herself of the few errant tears and said in a steady, confident voice, "Doc, I'm a nurse, remember? And I've given birth to four big babies. I can handle it." She looked at Michael and suggested, "Michael, why don't you help me hold still why the doctor works?"

Pops looked like he was about to protest when Mama looked at him with all the confidence she could muster and said firmly, "Because I need Herbert to hold my hand and talk to me. Okay, honey?"

Michael was sure this was the hardest thing he had ever had to do in his life. Mama was being a real trooper and nothing more than whimpers escaped her lips, but he could feel the horrible pain coursing through her as he held her firmly in place.

Michael had seen tears in his father's eyes before, but always they had been tears of joy. The ones he saw fall from his father's eyes now were ones that seemed to embody years of weariness and worry, finally releasing themselves from his ravaged soul. He was as worried about Pops as he was about Mama.

As Michael walked down the hall, reflecting on the trauma of the last two hours, he heard his name called. He realized it was coming from Ben's room. He eased the door open and peered in at Rachel.

"What's goin' on, Michael? Is Mama hurt or somethin'?"

Michael smiled inwardly that Rachel had called Maggie Mama, then walked into the room and sat heavily in the chair by the bed. He and Rachel had not said more than a few words to each other since the night she'd screamed at him to get out. He'd tried once, but Rachel had been her usual self and had refused to hear him out.

Rachel looked at the spent expression in Michael's eyes and didn't know what to do or say. All she had ever known was anger and hurt. She didn't know how to be kind to him like he was to her, like these people were to each other. That made her angry, so she snapped at him, "Would you stop lookin' like you lost your puppy and tell me what's goin' on?"

Michael raised his tired eyes to her face and she saw the anger flash in them as he got up, "Ask someone else, Rachel. I don't have the energy to endure your vile temper today, okay?"

Rachel reached out and grabbed his hand, "Okay, sorry. Stay, will you? I'll listen this time." She squeezed his hand and had the sudden urge to pull him closer to her.

Michael turned slowly, looking first at their linked hands, and then meeting Rachel's sparkling blue eyes with inquisitive, warm, brown ones. Their eyes held for a time, then Michael asked, "Your leg feeling better?"

"Yeah, a lot better, thanks. Now it's only twice as big as it's 'pose to be." Rachel laughed nervously and tried to drop Michael's hand, but he curled it securely around hers and held on.

Still looking into Rachel's eyes, Michael began, "Mama and Pops' group was attacked on the way back from the cabin this morning. Mama had an arrow deep in her shoulder, and we had to push it on through and sterilize the wound."

For the first time in Rachel's life she was speechless. Not because Mama had been hurt, which did bother her, but because Michael was still holding her hand and squeezing it gently as he talked. The combination of that, coupled with his honey-brown eyes looking straight into her soul was making her feel light headed.

Michael continued, "The village has been in an uproar ever since Pops left. It was like everything had been on hold just waiting to snap when he was out of sight. A lot of strange things keep happening. Let's just say it's been a tough week for all of us. Wouldn't you agree?" Michael was thinking back to Rachel and Jeremy's terrible night just a few days ago.

When Rachel didn't answer, Michael realized with some shock that she must finally be experiencing some of the sensations flowing between them. He followed her gaze down to their hands. He increased the pressure and watched her visibly flinch. He took his other hand and lifted her chin. The fear he saw there wasn't unlike the fear he had seen in her eyes when she was telling him about the wolverine. He whispered gently, "I would never hurt you, Rachel."

The utter vulnerability that he saw in her eyes made him want to wrap her safely in his arms and never let her go. Instead, he slowly lowered his lips to hers.

* * * *

Jeremy ran into the room, jumped up on the bed, winced a little from the pain in his back, then proceeded to cross his legs Indian-style. He didn't even notice Rachel's startled look or how quickly she had jerked away from Michael.

The little boy looked at Rachel with solemn eyes, a look much too mature for his three years. "Thank you for saving me from the monster."

Christina appeared in the doorway, breathless, and when her eyes met Jeremy's, she said, "Jeremy! I didn't mean you could come over here by yourself, you're still sick!"

"Am not!" He turned back to Rachel and ignored his mother. "It was going to eat me, wasn't it?"

Rachel was her old self again now that Michael wasn't messing her up, so she looked at Jeremy and stated, "Yeah, he woulda' ate you, but he's dead now and can't ever hurt you again. Don't be crawlin' out no more boards in the wall. You hear?"

When Jeremy nodded vigorously, Rachel added, "And he ain't no monster. He was just a hungry animal. You stay close to the big people, inside the walls, and no animals can get you in here."

"Do you promise?" Jeremy pleaded.

"Course I promise," Rachel stated firmly.

Satisfied that he had completed his mission with Rachel, Jeremy acknowledged Michael standing by the bed and lunged into his arms. Michael was saying, "Watch your back, Jeremy!" but too late the little boy realized his mistake. Michael caught him as gently as possible, but still received a loud, "Ouch!" from Jeremy.

Christina rushed over and lifted his shirt to see if any of the stitches had torn loose. She exclaimed, "Nothing came loose this time, but you're going home, do you hear me, young man?"

Rachel saw Jeremy look up at Michael and roll his eyes. From her privileged position on the bed she saw Michael acknowledge by rolling his eyes. It was clear Christina had missed the whole exchange. When Rachel looked at Michael again, he winked at her.

Looking at Rachel with a near worshiping expression on her face, Christina said, "How will I ever thank you, Rachel, for giving me my little boy back?" Tears rolled down her beautiful cheeks and her bright green eyes shone with sincerity.

Rachel couldn't have been more uncomfortable in a snake pit. Christina was all wet-faced hanging over her, Michael was still staring at her with that particular lopsided smile that made her stomach do flips, and that kid, he looked like he'd believe her if she told him the grass was purple. All of these things combined made her statement come out more harsh than she had intended, "You've already thanked me a million times. That's enough."

Christina looked embarrassed, cleared her throat and said in a tiny voice, "I'm sorry. I didn't mean to bother you."

Michael rushed to his sister-in-law's rescue. He shifted Jeremy carefully into his left arm and took Christina by the elbow with his right and began ushering her toward the door. Jeremy looked over Michael's shoulder and practically yelled at Rachel, "I wuv you, Rach!" In the next instant he turned back toward Christina and pleaded, "Mommy, please let me see Grandmama before we go home. Please!"

Christina nodded her okay, then started talking to Michael about Mama. Rachel felt as though she had suddenly disappeared under the rug and was thankful for it.

"Oh, Michael, I don't know how you did it," Christina said. "I don't think I could have held Mama while they...they hurt her like that. And I can't thank you enough for handling all the problems in the village while Pops was gone. Adam says you've saved him from a slow death. Michael, you know he just doesn't have it in him to be a leader like you and Pops. He used to be so miserable thinking he had to follow after Pops, he was a grouch! Now he's back to his normal, music-loving, free self. Thank you for giving him back to me." She smiled a smile of pure love for Adam, and finished by saying, "You know his music is all he ever cared to perform."

Michael thought again what a lucky man Adam was as he looked at Christina's angelic face filled with so much love for his big brother. Some people had all the luck. He couldn't even get a ragamuffin like Rachel to give him the time of day.

Michael turned to find her eyes intently studying the exchange between him and Christina. Why didn't she affect him like a ragamuffin? She certainly looked like one, didn't she? He kissed Jeremy on the cheek and handed him gingerly over to Christina. She reached up and gave Michael a smack on the jaw, and after giving Rachel one last look of gratitude, turned and left the room.

Michael just stood by the door and stared at Rachel, as

though he were studying a really interesting object, until she was so uncomfortable she decided to give him a little of his own treatment. Two could play his game. She met his eyes first, then looked him over from head to toe, slowly. She had intended to embarrass him, but what she got was a large grin that immediately lightened the mood.

Rachel asked, "What'd you do that for?"

"What?" Michael replied, still grinning.

"You know, what you did before Jeremy and his mother came in." Rachel's self-consciousness suddenly left her. She was so interested in his answer that she completely forgot about herself.

Michael's grin slid away and his look became serious again. "I'm not sure."

"You do that kind of thing a lot, then?"

Michael's reply came quickly, "No. Never."

His reply threw her off balance again, so she stated, "I guess it's been a weird week all the way 'round. Let's just call it stupid and forget it. That okay with you?"

The reply came much slower this time. "I'm not sure."

"Well. Anythin' you are sure about?" came Rachel's frustrated response. Embarrassment was lurking in the shadows again and that had her resorting to her usual anger as a cover up.

Michael lowered his eyes to her lips. When they raised to meet Rachel's eyes again they were filled with an odd kind of wonder, something that made Rachel's stomach start that silly flip-flopping again. "Only that I would like to do it again."

Now it was Rachel's turn to be slow in her reaction. She squirmed under his close scrutiny, but finally raised her chin and asked the question that was on her mind, "Why do you want to do it again?"

"You aren't going to like the answer," Michael grinned in spite of his better judgement.

"Let me guess. You ain't sure." Rachel found herself returning his grin.

"You should do that more often," Michael stated.

"Do what?"

"Smile. You're really pretty when you do. It kinda lights up your whole face." Michael smiled as the red crept into Rachel's cheeks. "Well, I need to get going. One disaster after another awaits my attention. Some of the kids have been setting booby traps and they're not being well received with all the commotion we've had around here the last few days, so I'm supposed to figure out something."

The red flag went up as soon as Michael mentioned Joe's favorite hobby. "What kind of booby traps?"

Michael replied, "You know, the regular stuff. Ropes tied to tree limbs snagging people's feet or throwing something rotten at them. Trip wires—some that just make you fall, others that release a small rock or something to whack you." The grin that had reappeared on Michael's face let Rachel guess that he'd had some fun with similar things himself.

"Stuff like that happen a lot?" Rachel wanted to know.

"No, I guess not. Pops usually handles problems like that, so I couldn't say for sure, but I think I would have heard about it. It is a pretty small place."

"That it is," Rachel rolled her eyes for emphasis.

"You really hate it here, don't you, Rachel?" Michael was incredulous.

"You sound like that's hard for you to believe," Rachel said just as incredulously.

Michael smiled, enjoying the fact that this little wisp of a woman could hold her own with him. After pondering it for a moment, he decided she could probably hold her own with about anything. Wolverines. Roughnecks. Naomi. He laughed out loud with that last vision.

"What, you idiot?" Rachel couldn't decide whether to be insulted or give in to the laughter that bubbled inside her for the first time in a long time. She decided there was no point in changing things now, she'd acted like a complete fool since meeting this man. Her laugh was tentative at first, until

Michael threw his head back and hooted. Then she laughed so hard that tears watered her eyes.

"Now, that really made a difference!" Michael exclaimed between laughs.

"What are you ramblin' about now?" smiled Rachel.

"You were pretty when you smiled, but you went beautiful on me when you laughed. You do that kind of thing a lot, then?" Michael threw her own favorite question back at her.

"No. Never." She held his eyes until he had to look away.

Michael cleared his throat and said, "Well, here's what I think. You just haven't been able to get a proper perspective regarding our fabulous village from that bed. What would you say to a full-scale guided tour by yours truly?" He bowed gracefully.

Rachel eyed him suspiciously, but the thought of getting out of bed and outside won hands down over any worry about his motives. She couldn't begin to hide her enthusiasm when she asked, "Can we do it now?"

Michael laughed and said, "That's what I had in mind. I could use a distraction myself before I have to get serious over booby traps." A frown suddenly creased his brow. "But your leg...."

"Don't even say it, Michael! Just get me a stick and I could hobble to the moon." Rachel's expression was that of a child who had been promised a lollipop and wasn't accepting any excuses for failing to deliver.

Within minutes they were on the front porch and Rachel was breathing deeply of the spring air. She noticed immediately that the rolling dust and the flies were almost nonexistent today, at least inside the village's walls. Had it been this way before? Michael took her elbow trying to help her down the steps while she balanced herself on the crutches.

The eager look in Rachel's eyes brought a smile to Michael's face. "What is your preference, my lady, the human side or the animal side first?"

"Definitely the animal side," Rachel said without hesitation.

"Don't tell me you've had enough of us humans."

Without any effort toward humor, Rachel answered, "I had enough of people a long time ago."

Michael tried to mask his dismay and disgruntlement over such a statement, but he must have done a poor job of it. Rachel glanced over at him and after the initial surprise spread across her face, her eyes sparked with anger. Michael would not be misunderstood this time, though. "Rachel, you get a hold on that demon temper right now! And don't put words into my mouth! What just made you so angry that your eyes almost ignited my hair?"

"I'll tell you what ignites me is your idiot faces when you hear somebody say somethin' that's different from you and your perfect little world. A person can turn into frog poop from one minute to the next by the look you get in your eyes. You really need to learn to play your cards." When Michael went blank, Rachel clarified, "You know, have a poker face once in a while so's somebody can at least imagine they're not frog poop to you."

Michael felt so frustrated that he wanted to hit something, instead he walked away and mumbled, "I wish you were frog...whatever, to me, it'd sure as heck be easier that way!"

Rachel watched Michael as he paced a tight circle and shook her head. Weird man. She'd never met a man that didn't just come out and say what he was thinking, and most times with his fists or something worse when he was as mad as Michael was. His courage must be a little on the scarce side despite his size.

When he finally walked back over to Rachel, his voice was calm, just like his whisper had been in her ear that first day after she'd kicked him. "I'm sorry if I insulted you with my eyes. I assure you that you are not frog...poop in my eyes. Now, would you like that tour?"

Rachel just gave an irate nod and started hobbling. When Michael tried to take her elbow, she jerked it away and spit, "I can walk by myself, Michael!"

Something about her calling him by his given name gave some acknowledgement to their relationship, whether she liked it or not. Whether he liked it or not. It made no sense, but he did like it.

When they reached the big barn and stepped inside, Rachel couldn't figure out why Michael was smiling. "What're you smilin' about? I swear if you ain't like a lizard, changin' from one minute to the next."

"I just...."

Rachel's exclamation cut Michael's response short, "Wow! How are you keepin' all these animals alive? I didn't think there were this many goats or chickens left in the whole country."

"Well, it's not easy. We work twenty-four hours a day here, in shifts, just to keep everything—and everybody—fed and cared for." Michael looked around proudly at the clean, neat, productive barn. "We recycle, use every bit of waste to nourish something else. The manure fertilizes the green houses and the restocking fields. The peelings and scraps from all the vegetables and the egg shells feed the chickens and the pigs. All of the adult animals feed their young, and us, with their milk, so the only up-front feed that we have to supply is the grain and hay for some of the adult animals we keep. Everything else, food for the other animals and most of ours, is a by-product."

Rachel was listening intently and had a hundred questions. "You make that sound so easy, but where do you get the grain and hay? If you haven't noticed, there is a famine in the land and the water and air are pretty much shot. There ain't nothin' much growin' out there."

"We had the huge overhead loft full of hay plus a building full of basic food stuffs and grain by the time all the families pitched in. When things got bad we all gathered here with our supplies and animals, built a wall, and greenhouses and constructed a restocking field in the back of the village."

Rachel fired another question immediately, "What's a

restocking field? If it's outside, it'd be poisoned."

"You're right, it would be. But it isn't completely outside. It had to be larger than any greenhouse we could build, to restock the hay and grain supplies for so many animals, so we made something in between. It's outside, but it's sheltered from the acid rain with special treated canvas and ditches all around to prevent runoff from coming into it. We have to repair, heat and light, water, cultivate and harvest it constantly, and we have to use gasoline generators and water filters. It's a lot of work, but it produces. Some villages have chosen to keep each family's production separate, but we voted to combine our efforts. It's not like there's a lot else for us to be doing right now anyway."

Rachel was already walking toward the back of the village when she asked, "Can we see it now?"

"Sure, but it's nothing pretty, just functional. We had no idea it would have to last this long."

Michael's weariness crept out for an instant, and Rachel saw it before he was able to hide it. "How long have you been gathered here?" Rachel queried as they walked.

"Six years, almost seven."

"You've been able to grow that much?" Rachel asked in awe.

"Well, we were able to stock more those first two years, we have another large house that we converted into a barn for storage over on the north side. We restock as much as possible, but we still have to use a steady amount of the storage. So far we're still keeping ahead, but it couldn't go on like this forever."

"How do you keep people from coming in here and taking it from you?" Rachel was really interested in hearing Michael's reply. She knew her men had been inside the walls, probably taking what they wanted in the middle of the night and setting booby traps to rub it in.

Michael became very solemn and looked Rachel in the eye when he answered, "We didn't build the walls just to keep the people out, Rachel. We've never turned anyone away who would follow the rules and standards of the village. We built the wall because we knew we could never endure watching what goes on out there when we could do nothing to change it, and, most importantly, we have always had a lot of help beyond our own."

Chapter 5

Sarah couldn't stand listening to them any longer. She had been sitting by the band's camp for almost an hour and the big morons didn't even know she was there. She had sat with Mama until she'd fallen asleep, then went for a walk to escape her own gloomy thoughts and had ended up here.

She had listened to Joe brag about the things he had taken from the village people and the tricks he had played on them. She had sat through Daniel's vivid rendition of how one of the village's young women undressed in front of her window while he was watching. He was convinced that she had done it on purpose for him. He sure thought highly of himself, didn't he?

William kept blubbering on about some imaginary girlfriend back home, wherever that was. Hadn't he always been with them? It sure seemed like it. And Troy. He just sat there and took it all in, not saying a word, except to give an occasional order to someone to do something. Why didn't he tell them they had to stop bothering the village people? Those good people gave them food every day and were taking care of her and Rachel. Why were they hurting them?

Dumb. Just plain dumb. She had to go talk to Rachel before the village people kicked them all out. She knew Rachel could lose her leg without the antibiotics.

Sarah skittered from behind the bush and headed back to the village gate. She didn't think she could stand being back with the band again. Her thoughts were heavy and sad. She pulled her borrowed sweater closer around her. The wind and dust were so much worse outside the village walls. She felt so safe in there, and so miserable out here.

As the village gate came into view up ahead, Sarah heard a familiar call, so she quickly turned and listened. Just a few feet away she saw William standing near a tree with his hands to his mouth making the call that sounded like an owl, two shorts and one long. After a few minutes, another figure seemed to melt away from a big oak just a few yards away from them. Sarah watched as William opened his beefy arms and the figure ran into them.

Sarah watched in fascination as William kissed the person in his arms. William, big dumb William, had a girl-friend?

William looked over the girl's shoulder right at Sarah and waved for her to come to him. After looking around to make sure no one else was around, it was pretty clear to Sarah that she had been discovered. But by William? She heard a confirmation, "Come on over here and meet Ginny, Sarah." William was trying to whisper loudly, but his whisper would soon shake the village, so Sarah hurried over to them.

William turned the girl around to Sarah, shoved her forward a step and said proudly, "This is my Ginny, Sarah. I don't want the others to know about her, okay, 'cause I'd have to hurt them over her. So don't be tellin' them, okay?"

Sarah looked into the face of the pretty oriental girl and smiled. "You know I wouldn't tell them anythin', William. How did ya'll meet?"

"We met on the road a while back. Ginny's granny died, so Ginny follows along behind us now, she's real good at it. Then I volunteer for night patrol every night so I can be with Ginny. Nobody cares, not even Troy. I tell him I can't sleep. He's just glad he don't have to stay up. Me and Ginny take turns staying awake and watchin'. You won't tell will you, Sarah?"

"'Course not. I told you I wouldn't. Does Rachel know?" asked Sarah.

"She ain't said nothing. But I think she knows. You can tell her if you want to." William suddenly looked worried. "Rachel won't make her leave, will she, Sarah?"

"Let me talk to her, okay?" Sarah patted William on the arm and said, "It'll be all right." She wasn't at all sure it would be, though. Rachel had decided years ago, after William came, that she wouldn't allow anyone else to join them. She had said they could barely feed and watch out for themselves, and more people just made it worse.

William looked at Sarah's hand on his arm and smiled. "You're getting jus' like them villagers, ain't you Sarah? I think that's just real good. And you got a boyfriend too, don't you?"

Sarah dropped her hand from William's arm and asked, "What boyfriend?"

"Ah, you know who I'm talkin' 'bout, Sarah. Don't you play games with me. I'm not that dumb." He gave Sarah a big, dumb grin, and that, coupled with his rapidly reddening cheeks made him look like a painted clown, big ears and all.

Ginny piped in with her broken English, "His name Ben!"

Sarah sputtered, "He's not my boyfriend! Where'd you get that idea?"

"He look at you like William look at me," smiled Ginny.

"He does?" Sarah asked with a startled voice.

William and Ginny both nodded vigorously.

"Well, I gotta get back. Ya'll take care, and don't let Joe see you. Especially Joe." Sarah instructed.

Ginny rushed over and gave Sarah a big hug, then ran back to William's arms.

Sarah looked back and waved several times. William had a girlfriend, and according to them, she had a boyfriend. It was too bad they were wrong about that. She had her fist raised to knock on the gate when it opened suddenly and Ben appeared in the archway. "Sarah, I can't believe you're out here again by yourself. It'll be dark soon. You know all you have to do is ask me and I'll be glad to come with you. What are you doing, anyway?"

Sarah stared at him for a minute, then blurted, "It ain't none of your business, and 'sides, you don't have any time for me. You're always with your girlfriends."

"My girlfriends!" Ben laughed. "How many girlfriends do you think I have?"

"I don't think you have any, really. You're too ugly. But you pretend like you do," scoffed Sarah.

"And why would I do that?" Ben was still laughing.

Sarah was quiet for a minute, just staring at Ben until he stopped laughing. She said quite sadly, "'Cause you're afraid you might have to be 'round me."

Ben's color raised a shade or two and he made a big show of kicking at the dust rolling around his feet. He stopped suddenly, stared at Sarah's face that was showing so much hurt, then grabbed her and pulled her into his arms. She was swallowed up in his massive frame. He lowered his head down to her, almost stooping to get to her because she was so short, and kissed her tenderly on the cheek.

"I am afraid of you, tidbit, but it's not for the reasons you're thinking." Ben wanted to explain, but he was having a hard time putting something into words that he didn't understand himself.

Sarah didn't know what came over her, but she raised herself up on her tiptoes and pulled Ben's head to hers and kissed him squarely on the lips. She had intended for it to be a quick, brave statement that she wasn't a baby, no tidbit. But his lips were so soft and warm, and he smelled so good. Her arms went around his neck and her fingers ran through his beautiful tawny hair as he leaned into the kiss.

Just as suddenly, he jerked her arms from around his neck and pushed her back a step. "What did you do that for, Sarah! Goodness, what if somebody sees us. They'd think I was taking advantage of a kid. I can't deal with this! Go home! I'll see you later."

Sarah watched in stunned silence as Ben slammed the gate shut, gave the guards in the tower a worried glance, then stomped off. Ever so slowly a smile began to form on Sarah's lips. Maybe she did have a boyfriend! He just didn't know it yet. He was chicken. He was a coward. She knew all about being a coward. But not this time. Not this time.

She took it slow walking back to the house. Their house. Not her house. She didn't have a house, or mother and father. She just had Rachel. And Daniel. And she guessed she had Troy, Joe and William whether she liked it or not. And Ginny. She was still half-smiling when she stepped up on the porch.

"It's nice this time in the evening, just before dark, wouldn't you say?" asked Pops.

"Goodness sakes," exclaimed Sarah. "I didn't see you there, you scared the pants off me!"

Pops gave a hearty laugh at the picture Sarah had just painted in his mind. He loved to listen to the girls talk. They could really tell a story! "Well, I just saw Ben stomping by, so I figured you'd be somewhere close behind."

"Why would you figure that?" Sarah asked as straight-faced as possible.

"Well, it's like this, Sarah. That boy's been in a tither for some time now, and it seems to get real concentrated when you're nearby." Against his better judgement, Pops hooted. It felt good to get his mind off of Maggie for a few minutes.

"That's 'cause I just kissed him! He's a coward," Sarah stated flatly.

Pops eyebrows raised, "Say you just kissed him? Do you mind if I ask how old you are, Sarah?"

"I'm almost eighteen, why?" Sarah surprised herself again by squaring her shoulders and raising her chin a notch or two.

Pops hooted again. "Everyone thought you were much younger! But I should have known better. It takes a woman to tell a story like you do! And to get Ben so riled up." He thought about Ben's face as he'd walked by a minute ago, slapped his knee and hooted again. As soon as he settled down, he patted the chair next to him and said, "Come and sit with me, Sarah. We have some talking to do while Mama's resting."

* * * *

"That's the second time you've bragged 'bout your big, bad army. So where are they?" Rachel somehow managed to put both her hands on her hips around the crutches and stood waiting defiantly for Michael's answer.

"My what?"

"All your help you brag about all the time. The help you had beyond your own when you captured us," Rachel mocked. "And all the help you have keepin' this place safe."

Michael cleared his throat, embarrassed that she still didn't understand, and motioned toward the greenhouses. "Want to see the greenhouses first, since they're on the way to the restocking fields?"

Rachel nodded and decided to let him avoid her question for now, but she would sure as heck find out where his help was, and she knew just who to ask. She had to get word to Troy so they wouldn't play around and get ambushed by Michael's other men. They wouldn't be prepared for that. It seemed Michael had a few secrets. She eyed his tall frame with his long dark hair and couldn't decide whether to admire his cunning or take one of her crutches and knock him down.

They stepped inside the first, biggest, greenhouse and Rachel lost all previous concerns. "Holy cow, Michael! Is this a turnip?" Rachel took her finger and dug just a little dirt away from the green top and smiled in delight as the round white and purple bulb appeared.

"Yep, that's what it is. Go ahead, pull it and we'll cut it up." Michael was pulling out his pocket knife as he spoke.

Rachel gave the green top a yank without hesitation. She loved turnips and thought she'd never get to taste another one. The root plants were the first to go when the soil started dying. She watched in anticipation as Michael shook the dirt from the perfectly round bulb and began peeling it.

Glancing up and seeing Rachel's face suddenly made all the hours and hours he'd put into growing those dang turnips worth every minute of it; the root crops were the hardest to grow inside. He handed a thick slice to her with a smile.

After hungrily devouring that slice and eagerly taking a huge bite from another, Rachel groaned out loud and said, "I think I done died and gone to heaven!" She started walking through the aisles in wonderment. She fingered the tender feathers of the carrot tops and radishes, reverently stared at the leaf lettuce and squeaked with joy over the sign that read CORN. "Will it be coming up soon?"

"Yes. We start it inside and then transplant it in the field. That's the only way we can get it to grow. Do you like corn?" Michael prompted, wanting to hear more of her excited exclamations.

"Naw. Not me so much. It's Sarah that loves corn. Has she seen all this?" Rachel made a sweep with one hand and continued to stare in awe around the greenhouse.

"Are you kidding! Sarah stays out here most of the time. She and Mama are always out here helping and talking. They get along real well." Michael had beamed his information, sure that Rachel would be happy that Sarah was doing so well in the village.

Well, maybe not. There it was again, that stubborn look that came into Rachel's eyes when she was mad about something. This time it was quickly replaced with hurt and then fear. Michael stared in fascination at the play of emotions that passed across this woman's unique features. Such a beautiful little thing to be so angry, so unhappy. Michael wished he could make her happy, help her to experience some joy and peace in her life. He shivered when he realized just how much he wanted to do those things for her.

How could he begin to share the things that really meant something to him, the things that made all the turmoil and uncertainty bearable? Rachel would laugh at him and make fun of his beliefs. She would call him a dreamer and an idiot. When he realized again how deeply he wanted to touch her heart, to have her understand with him, it scared him. It would be a dumb thing to lay his heart open to this woman.

She was not one of them; she hated them and their prissy ways. The unwanted thought popped into his head: Rachel is a heathen, pure and simple.

Rachel looked up and saw Michael staring at her with that you-poor-dumb-thing look and almost hit him square in the jaw. Instead, she got a tight rein on herself and vowed to reclaim Sarah from these people, people who looked down their noses at others who were different. She didn't doubt the other villages were the same. No wonder there were people still outside.

The cold resignation came through in her voice when she spoke, "My leg's gettin' pretty tired, guess we better finish up so I can get off it for a while."

Michael sighed, recognizing that their short truce had just ended, not really knowing why. Why was he surprised? Nothing had changed, he never knew why with Rachel. Now why was that? He took the chance of making her even madder by standing and pondering that for a moment, wanting desperately to say or do something that would change the disastrous pattern developing between them. The thought that suddenly came to his mind floored him. Kiss her. It's the only way you will be able to convince her you really don't believe what you were just thinking. It showed all over your face and in your eyes. Perhaps you are the heathen.

Rachel admitted to herself that Michael looked at her sometimes like her father used to look at her, with repulsion. Well, then she'd just handle him the same way.... Oh, no, Michael was moving toward her and he wasn't looking at her with repulsion. It was that other look, the one that made her stomach hurt.

Michael swallowed to rid himself of the knot that had formed in his throat. He had never ignored inspiration before, he wasn't going to start now, even if it had slapped him in the face. He wondered if he would get another slap for following it. He walked around the table where Rachel stood waiting impatiently for him. He reached down slowly and took her hands in his, never taking his eyes from hers.

Rachel steeled herself. She would not allow him to treat her like this. One minute he looked at her like she was trash, the next treasure. Which one was she? She couldn't believe he was making her question herself, she would just.... Oh, no, he was going to do it again.

Just as Michael leaned down to kiss her he vowed it would never be this way again. He had to kiss her now to show her that she was as good as he was, even though they were completely and incurably different. The next time he taught Rachel he would be explaining to her that she, or any woman, is better than any man's kiss. He certainly would not be forcing his own on her.

As she began to melt under his tender kiss, something opened inside her that challenged her to fight back. She did the only thing he wouldn't expect, she instinctively used the only power she possessed to weaken him, though she had never used it before. Rachel dropped the crutches, put both arms around Michael's neck and stretched up on her tip toes to return the kiss.

Several minutes later, Michael pulled away from Rachel. He sat down hard with his legs folded beneath him and tried to control his breathing. He looked at Rachel, taking in her mussed hair and clothing, and he was filled with shame. "Oh, Rachel, I'm sorry. I didn't mean...."

She raised her hand to stop his words as she sat down beside him. "I know. I didn't expect that to happen either." Rachel decided to be completely honest. "I just thought I'd pay you back for torturing me, but I think...well, I tortured myself more." She looked away.

Michael blurted, "No, that isn't possible! You won. I am definitely tortured. I deserved that, but you didn't. Please, will you forgive me...and promise me you'll help me to never do that again."

Rachel's face turned red and she tried to reach for her crutches to get away from him before he said more cruel things. Michael snatched up the crutches and threw them across the aisle to the other side of the greenhouse in a very unusual fit of frustration. He turned to Rachel and found her fists raised, ready to defend herself.

Once again ashamed of his actions, Michael took in a deep, cleansing breath and gently pushed Rachel's fists back to her sides. "Not this time, Rachel. You're not steaming off until we talk this through. I did not mean what I just said as an insult. No woman has ever made me feel...and want...more than you just did. That is a compliment. Do you understand?"

"Then why don't I feel complimented?" Rachel lowered her eyes, trying to believe him.

"Because what I...we...just did is not the right way to express the attraction we feel for each other." Michael lifted Rachel's chin and looked into her eyes.

She stared back with so many questions blazing in the depths of her gaze. "Why? You said it felt good, didn't you?"

Michael sighed and looked away for a minute until he could think of the right way to say what he was thinking. "Rachel, it felt better than anything we have the right to be sharing with each other."

"Why?"

"Because we have not committed ourselves to each other in marriage. We would be playing around with the most marvelous power ever given to man, purely for pleasure."

Rachel frowned, "So you're tellin' me the pleasure part is wrong, dirty?"

Michael's eyes drifted over Rachel and once again he felt a passion so overwhelming that he was shaken down to his soul. He wanted to tell her what a beautiful, pure thing love was supposed to be, the kind his parents and Adam and Christina had, but he wasn't feeling very pure. He looked away and spoke so quietly she could barely hear him, "No, it's not dirty—or wrong—if the circumstances are right."

Rachel was beginning to like this new-found power she seemed to have over Michael. She had truly enjoyed the feelings and sensations she'd felt while he was holding her. She had never allowed anyone to touch her before, except Troy.

She reached over and stroked Michael's hair and reveled in the shiver that embraced him simply because she had touched him.

"Please don't do that right now, Rachel."

When he did not seem to have the courage to look at her, she felt empowered to continue. She dropped her hand to his shoulder and used her fingertip to trace the muscular cord that ran down his neck. She scooted closer and put the other hand on his thigh. The quake that streaked through him was of such fierce force that she jerked her hand away in reaction.

He raised his eyes to hers then, and the longing she saw there reminded her of a hungry child's gaze before a table full of delicious food.

"Ah, excuse me...Michael are you in need of a chaperon?" Adam's eyes alternated between mirth and worry. The worry soon won the battle when Michael didn't get up right away and Rachel didn't look embarrassed.

When Michael finally stood and helped Rachel to her feet, he was slow to turn and acknowledge his brother. "Adam, would you hand me those crutches over there, please?" Michael continued to hold Rachel's arm until her crutches arrived. Once she was securely balanced on them again, Michael looked fully at his brother and asked, "Will you please continue the tour of the village with Rachel? I'm sorry, but I can't continue right now and I promised it to her."

"Sure, I can do that. Where are you off to?" Adam asked as casually as he could manage. He was still in shock at the scene he had just witnessed. Straight-as-an-arrow Michael, the-next-leader-of-the-village Michael, making out in the hay in broad daylight with an outsider who wore men's clothing and limped from a round in the woods with a wolverine? Naw. He must be dreaming.

"I don't know. Thanks, Adam. See you later, Rachel." Michael wandered off with his hands in his pockets, never looking back.

Adam watched Michael's retreat and almost missed the

triumphant smile that crossed quickly over Rachel's lips.

He cleared his throat and asked, "Well, are you still up for the rest of that tour, Rachel?" He was wondering why she was out hobbling around on her leg—it had to hurt—but he just shook his head when he recalled the scene he'd walked in on and realized he was wondering about more serious things than this little woman's leg. He was really concerned about Michael. He knew how badly Michael wanted a family. He was lonely. Adam made a mental note to see if he couldn't hurry that reality along. He knew the perfect young woman, she had always been Christina's favorite pick for Michael. Adam's brother had just been working too hard. He would speak to Pops about it tonight.

Rachel answered Adam for the second time and finally got his attention, "I wouldn't miss it."

"I'm sorry, Rachel. My mind drifted off for a minute. Shall we?" Adam let Rachel lead the way.

Adam and Rachel had barely spoken to each other, so their conversation was sparse and a bit of tension lingered between them. Both were still thinking about what had happened between her and Michael and what it might mean. Once they walked into the research lab all other thoughts and concerns disappeared. Rachel's enthusiasm and interest in the experiments soon drew Adam into the excitement.

"So you've actually figured out how to make pure water?"

Rachel was so animated, so electrified that Adam laughed out loud. "Well, no, not exactly. I don't think anyone but God can actually create a lot of water, but Pops and Michael have discovered that pure water flows through the connection occasionally. We never know when it's going to happen, though, so someone has to monitor and test constantly. The miraculous thing is that the pure water, in the correct proportions, eats up the contagion in our stored water without the complicated and slow reverse-osmosis process.

"Have you told the people on the outside about it?

They're all bein' poisoned," Rachel challenged. "Most of 'em don't have a filter."

"We'd like to, we really would," Adam defended. "But it's not that simple. We barely get enough pure water to treat the village's water, and the pure water doesn't work it's magic on the water outside the village anyway. We've tried so many times. It's just a gift to us, pure and simple."

"So that's why Michael got in such a snit about the connection we disabled," Rachel muttered. She'd known there was something special about that place, it had drawn her back every time she had tried to leave.

Adam didn't miss the comment and couldn't resist asking the question that had plagued his whole family, "Why did you do that?"

Rachel looked at the tall, handsome man who looked exactly like his father. He didn't have Michael's honey-brown eyes, but everything else clearly showed that they shared the same blood. She looked away as she told the half-truth, "We were just fillin' our jugs."

Adam knew a lie for what it was, but decided not to press the issue. Besides, he was actually having fun with Rachel, seeing the village in a new light through her eyes. "Want to see some more?"

Rachel's face lit up as she answered, "You bet I do! What now?"

By the time they were finished, Rachel was truly impressed. She had been shown all the storehouses of grain and dried goods, along with all the research that accompanied each facet of their survival in the village. It was complete, from which grinder worked the best for which grain to making soap that smelled good and to the regulation of the compost pile. She saw the schedules that insured that the village projects ran smoothly, that each family did their fair share and had time left for their own family operations. She was surprised at how much of it was supervised by Pops and Michael. They seemed to be intricately involved in everything.

Rachel couldn't believe they even had a washhouse that accommodated the whole village's laundry with its own massive schedule. The sign above the door had read, CLEAN-LINESS IS NEXT TO GODLINESS. "Who runs this?" Rachel had asked. She had found out then that every family had a time assigned to them. They would do their own family's laundry, plus some extra for the elderly or sick. She had looked on the schedule and found every adult member of Michael's family in a slot for the upcoming month. It looked like they took turns and shared the load. Sarah's name had also been in a slot, and that had brought a frown to Rachel's brow.

As they approached the front steps of the house after the tour was complete, Naomi came flying out the front door. "Hi, you guys! What's going on?"

Adam grabbed Naomi and messed up her hair, laughing when she slugged him in the chest. "I've just been giving Rachel a tour of the village."

"Why, where's Michael?" Naomi waited innocently for Adam's reply.

After exchanging a careful glance with Rachel, Adam answered, "He had something he had to do, so he asked me to finish the tour he'd started with Rachel. I just happened by at the right time."

Rachel thought how wrong Adam's timing had been and a smile tugged at the corner of her mouth.

Naomi wondered what was really going on, but was in too big of a hurry to care right then. "Well, I gotta go let Christina get a few more measurements for the wedding dress and then I've got to change and be off to do some work in the barn." She turned back around as if having a second thought, "Adam, please tell Pops that Michael is working too much. He's too weird lately. Okay?"

"I hear you, Sis. I was planning on talking to him about that very thing tonight anyway, so consider it done."

Naomi nodded. "Bye, Rachel." She tossed over her shoulder, "Mama's okay. She's resting."

"See ya." Rachel frowned as she stared longingly at the beautiful white sweater with matching gray slacks and turtleneck that Naomi modeled so naturally. She wondered why Naomi had said Michael was acting weird. Did she know what she and Michael had been doing?

Adam saw the longing so clearly on Rachel's face and shook his head in silent marvel as he remembered why he had gone in search of Michael and Rachel in the first place. So that's why Naomi had slipped him a wink. Christina was waiting and was probably getting impatient by now.

Well, it wasn't every day that Adam popped in on his younger brother and found him doing things that made him seem like a younger brother for the first time in his life. It had rattled him and he had forgotten. Gee, he still didn't know where Michael was and he was supposed to bring him along, too. Christina was going to kill him for messing up her surprise.

Chapter 6

Rachel couldn't believe she had let Adam talk her into this. She was really tired, and her leg throbbed like that toothache she had a few years back. All she wanted to do was lie down on Ben's wonderfully soft bed and nurse her leg. And maybe her heart. Instead, she was limping to Adam's house because Christina said there was something she had to show her. She cringed as she thought of the flashy redhead who would be sappy with affection for her. She was sorry she'd ever gotten involved with these people. They were going to break her heart and she was letting them.

Adam opened the door for Rachel, sincerely hoping Christina knew what she was doing. Rachel looked like she was ready to kill something and he wasn't at all sure what he would do if she attacked his beautiful, sweet wife. He would just make sure he stood close enough to restrain her if it came to that.

Just as Rachel was wondering why the house was so dark, many voices shouted, "Happy Birthday" while candles and lanterns erupted into light. Rachel watched in shock as Michael's family blew little whistles at her and threw long, thin pieces of paper at her. Before she could form a logical thought, Mama latched onto her with her one good arm and was ushering her over to a table where a huge chocolate cake was shimmering with tons of candles. In the midst of it all, it vaguely registered that Mama should still be in bed, but Rachel's attention was captured by the cake. It had *Happy 22nd Birthday Rachel* written on top in beautiful white letters.

"What makes you think my birthday's today?" Rachel

asked Mama in a small voice.

From her usual tag-along position at Mama's side, Sarah appeared and poked her head over Rachel's shoulder and stated, "I found it written on one of the pages in the book we found after the fire. I've kept it all this time. I know when mine and Daniel's is, too."

Everyone waited in dead silence, even the children were without sound. Rachel looked around the room with its festive decorations, at all the faces peering at her, wondering why Adam was staying so close to her. Then she looked back to the table that held the cake, along with other delicious looking food and several wrapped presents. A small smile began to form at one corner of her mouth as she looked at Sarah and asked, "All this is for me?"

When Sarah nodded, Rachel's whole face blossomed into a wide-eyed, childish grin and the whole room cheered "Hurray!" and broke into a full rendition of the happy birthday song. When Christina and Adam told her she had to make a wish before she could blow the candles out and eat the cake, Rachel's eyes automatically searched the room to see if Michael was there. Just when she was feeling the dumbest for having even thought of him, Rachel's eyes met Adam's and held for a long moment before she managed to ask, "Out loud?"

The twins, Amy and Paul, were standing on their tiptoes peering over the edge of the table ogling the goodies. They shouted, first Amy, "No! Silly." Then Paul, "It won't come true if we hear it!"

Rachel looked down at her toes, and just when everyone thought the party was about to take a turn for the worst and they were going to get a taste of her vile temper again, Rachel grinned at the twins and began to speak in perfect German before blowing the candles out with a fantastic trill that sounded like a chorus of baby birds. Everyone laughed and the twins shouted "Wow" just as Jeremy catapulted into Rachel's arms and sent her crutches crashing to the floor, Rachel almost going with them.

She was still wooling his head and calling him a scala-wag in an unusual show of good humor when she noticed Michael by the door, grinning. She was having so much fun she didn't bother to hide her pleasure at seeing him there, so she returned his grin with one of her own. Just as she was easing Jeremy back to his feet, being careful with his back, Christina walked over and put her arm around Rachel and motioned toward the presents. "Open your gifts, Rachel. We just completed them a few minutes ago. Whew, we thought we weren't going to get them finished!"

Rachel looked into Christina's eyes and saw something genuine there and it truly made her feel good. A little embarrassed with her new emotions, Rachel looked at the clinging baby Jeremiah in Christina's arms, and for lack of anything else to do, held out her arms to him on impulse. Christina was just about to explain that Jeremiah never went to anyone, when the baby leaned into Rachel's arms and then snuggled into her shoulder with his thumb in his mouth.

As the collective gasp grew in the room, the twin Paul verbalized for everyone, "Well, what'a ya know, baby Jeremiah ain't never done that before!"

"Hasn't ever done that before," Christina corrected, then smiled at Rachel and said, "It's a miracle! I can't believe it. Do you want to take him home with you?"

As everyone joined in the laughter, Rachel's eyes drifted toward the door and was strangely relieved to see that Michael was still there watching. Her eyes met his for just one triumphant moment before the children demanded again that she open the presents. Adam offered to take the baby but Rachel just held him tighter and asked instead that he help her with the wrapping paper. She sat down in a chair that Ben brought over to her, and as she grabbed one side of the paper while Adam grabbed the other, she instructed, "On the count of three, okay?"

Adam laughed and said, "You got it!"

Jeremy rushed over and demanded that he get to rip the next one open, so Rachel said, "Okay, but wait just a minute and don't rip your back too, all right?" Jeremy waited patiently while Rachel lifted the beautiful sky-blue dress from the box. The material shimmered like azure lake water under a full moon. Rachel held it up in front of her and could see that it had a round scooped neckline with three-quarter length sleeves and that it came just below her knees. It was the tiniest, slinkiest, most beautiful thing she'd ever seen.

The next box held a crocheted sweater that was a delicate blend of white and the same color blue as the dress. The third box held a pair of soft leather flats that had a tiny border of handsewn flowers in the same hue of blue. Rachel had never been given a present before, these were her first. She suddenly realized she had spoken her thoughts aloud when the twin Amy shouted, "Well, you made out good, didn't ya?"

Rachel heard Michael hoot a loud, brawny laugh from the doorway and was helpless against joining in. Pops and Ben grabbed Amy and swung her by both arms until she cried "uncle" and swore she'd behave. The whole thing, her first party, had been so much fun until a beautiful platinum-haired woman joined Michael at the door and he began to talk to her in earnest. Rachel's angry eyes left them and immediately clashed into Adam's pensive ones, so when Naomi walked over to her and whispered, "Let's go in and put those things on you and that wonderful little figure of yours will make him forget all about Ms. Whitehead, what do you say?" Rachel had immediately grinned and said, "Let's do it."

Now she was really sorry she had agreed to put these fancy things on. The dress fit so perfectly that she could only take small steps and it made the bandage on her leg look ridiculously big. The dang shoes were so soft she was afraid they were going to fall apart. The sweater made her feel like she had fluffy clouds wrapped around her shoulders and Naomi had insisted on putting her hair up in one of those puffy messes like she wore. She had even insisted she wear lipstick, mascara on her thick lashes and some pearl earrings that belonged to Christina. All in all, she felt like a fool.

When she hobbled into the kitchen where everybody

was enjoying the food except her, everything fell silent for a moment, but then the low whistles started with everyone exclaiming how beautiful she looked. For the first time in her life, Rachel actually began to feel beautiful. Her eyes moved to the doorway and met Michael's. What she saw there gave her the courage to raise her chin a notch and limp with confidence she'd lacked a moment before. It was as though he read her thoughts and they exchanged a crooked smile before she turned toward the table for some of the cake she'd been anticipating all evening.

After Adam watched the last round of exchanged smiles between Michael and Rachel—the reformed Rachel that had even made him give a little whistle—he decided it was time to step up his plans. Christina and Naomi would lay awake and worry over their part in this whole mess if they knew what he knew.

"Michael, would you mind going over to the barn and checking on the white goat by the water barrels? She acted like she might deliver tonight and Christina will kill me if I leave right now."

The beautiful Karyn standing by Michael volunteered, "I'll go with you, Michael, and keep you company."

Michael grinned at Adam and said, "Well, how can I refuse that offer?"

Adam smiled in satisfaction as the two left together. They would make a good couple and Christina and Naomi loved her. He felt better already.

The delicious bite of cake she had just stuffed in her mouth suddenly lost its appeal when Rachel looked up just in time to see Michael take the showy white-haired woman by the arm and walk out the door. "Don't worry about her, Rachel, she has beautiful hair and she's nice enough, but she has no spunk. Michael would fall asleep on their wedding night." After Naomi whispered her secret in Rachel's ear, she started to walk off, but Rachel pulled her back.

"What makes you think I'm worried?" Rachel asked irritably.

One of Naomi's brows arched just like her brother's. "I speak German." When she saw Rachel turn pale, she was kind enough to add, "It was nice to hear it again since nobody else in the village knows it. My best friend back home was from Germany, and she taught me her native language and we spoke it together for years. It was our special thing."

Somewhat relieved, Rachel smiled at Naomi, admitting to herself that she liked Michael's sister whether she wanted to or not. Now it seemed they had a secret together. After Naomi walked away, Rachel's eyes drifted around the room and met with Adam's again. They weren't hostile. Protective, maybe. She guessed they had a secret, too.

Once her eyes left Adam they met with Christina's which were also studying her. Rachel smiled and Christina took it as an invitation, walking over to her. Baby Jeremiah immediately reached for Rachel and she automatically took him and neatly deposited him on her hip while leaning her crutch against the table with one fluid motion.

With a look of disbelief, Christina stated, "Well, it looks like you have had plenty of experience with children."

"Yeah, I guess so. Seems like I've toted Sarah and Daniel around all of my life," Rachel reflected.

"What's Daniel like, Rachel? How old is he?" Christina sincerely wanted to know more about the woman who had saved her son. She hadn't really paid attention to the fact that Rachel had a brother, too. She wondered if he was as sweet as Sarah.

"Oh, he's sixteen. Acts like he's twelve sometimes." Rachel looked away and sighed. When she looked back at Christina, the many years of responsibility for a younger brother and sister in a frightening world showed in her young eyes. "It's pretty weird to be lookin' up at him these days. He's over six feet now. Don't know where he got it. Everybody's short but him." Rachel gave a shrug.

Christina exclaimed, "Good grief! I just had the most horrible vision listening to you. Can you imagine a six-foot Jeremy!"

Rachel and Christina laughed as they recalled three-year-old Jeremy smearing cake icing all over the cat just an hour earlier. When Adam stopped him and told him to explain why he was doing that to the cat, he had stared down his frustrated daddy like he was one foot tall instead of his towering six feet three inches, put his hand on his hip and stated flatly, "I am being cre-ate-ive. Mom don't like this cat and she's gonna pitch him out if I don't do somethin'. She said so. If I make him chocolate, she'll like him, 'cause she loves chocolate. Now do you understand, Daddy?" His imitation of Rachel and Sarah's speech patterns had been almost perfect.

Christina was still smiling when she asked her next question, but she was actually quite concerned for Rachel. How in the world had she managed out there with two little siblings? "Surely Daniel is not as active in strange pursuits as our Jeremy, is he?"

Rachel started to spill all that concerned her about her relationship with her brother, like his constant challenges toward her authority and his relentless insults and aggression toward Sarah. Those things required her to call him down way too often for them to be on any kind of friendly terms. She knew the day was close at hand when their fighting would necessarily involve Troy in her defense. Daniel was just too big and strong for her to control any longer and she could not allow him to take over; he was simply too angry and had no feeling for fairness. She looked at Christina sadly and said, "Let's just say his pursuits are definitely active."

Christina could feel Rachel's bone-deep weariness over her brother and knew that she had to do something to help. She would talk to Adam and Michael tonight about bringing Daniel into the village so they could help with him. "Well, it'll get better when he gets out of those crazy teen years. I was a little crazy myself when I was sixteen. Hey, come on in the bedroom and let's get you out of those clothes and back into something comfortable so you and Mama can go home and get into bed before you both keel over."

Christina ushered Rachel into the bedroom and closed the door. Rachel had never been so happy to undress in her life. Her leg was really throbbing now and her spirits had crashed when Michael left with the white-head. Christina unzipped Rachel's dress for her and asked, "What's really bothering you, honey? You look like you...how is it you say it? Like you've lost your puppy?"

Rachel grinned, "I guess I do have a lot of sayin's."

"We love them all, too! You know you're the only exciting thing that's happened to this village in a very long time, and wow! I mean it has been exciting. Granted, it wasn't all your doing, you didn't plan on chasing a wolverine through the woods or agitating Michael out of his coma."

Rachel looked at Christina quizzically.

Christina didn't give her time to form the denial. "Listen, Rachel, save your breath with me. I'd know that look you're carrying around anywhere. I've had it on my face for years."

Rachel couldn't help but grin, "And what look is that?"

"The I'm-in-love-with-a-Rock look. Mama has it, I have it, and now you and Sarah have it. You might as well learn to deal with it, their perfect family and all, because it won't go away, it only gets worse." She added with a grin, "Or better, is more accurate."

Rachel didn't get a chance to respond, because Mama knocked on the door.

Mama walked toward her and Rachel could see that she looked as haggard as she herself felt. "I'm bushed, Rachel. You look pretty tired too. Do you want to walk home with me, honey?"

"Okay,...I guess." Rachel hedged. The truth was she still felt uncomfortable with this queen bee and her calling everybody, "Honey." Rachel recalled her vow to get Sarah away from her before she broke her heart. Rachel spit out her next statement a little more nastily than she had intended, "You should never've got out of bed today anyhow."

"Well, I couldn't miss your party. I've never missed one

of my children's parties, and I'm not going to start now." Mama looked at Rachel with true affection, "Come on, let's go. The men want to stay longer, but us cripples need to stick together."

It sounded like they had a secret, too. Only Rachel had no idea what it was.

That night Christina had tried to convince Adam and Michael that Rachel needed help with her brother and he should be brought into the village to live with them. Adam had flatly refused, giving all kinds of lame excuses, and muttering something about her not understanding the whole picture. Then he reminded her that Rachel had said she was leaving in a few days as soon as her leg had healed a little because she literally hated it in the village. Michael had just listened quietly, which was totally unlike him, so she went right over their heads to the one person they wouldn't dare argue with. Mama.

Mama and Christina thought they had the rooming arrangements all worked out between their two houses, each having four bedrooms. They could put Rachel and Sarah in Naomi's room, since Naomi wanted to work on her wedding dress more anyway, and could share Amy's room at Christina's house. Michael and Ben could share Ben's room and Daniel could have Michael's room.

It was all settled until Sarah went to get Daniel and came back with his refusal to leave Troy, Joe and William. There had been no way to get that many people crammed into their houses, so Pops and Mama had put their heads together and came up with the lean-to idea. It had been intended for the three extra men, but Rachel and Daniel had insisted they preferred to stay outdoors with them. It was what they were used to, after all.

Michael and Pops sat on the porch discussing the schedule changes for the next day, enjoying the unusually warm April weather, but they were having a hard time concentrating. The big lean-to across the street had been buzzing with activity as Rachel and her band set up camp under the protection of the big army canvas. They seemed to be settling down now; it was late and the little dark-haired man named Joe had finally finished up the dishes that he had let out a stream of profanities about. It seemed that it had been William's turn to cook and he had burned two of the pots, making Joe's job a long, messy one.

Even Pops leaned forward in consternation when the older bearded man, Troy, rolled out his blankets and stood patiently waiting until Rachel came and joined him. She arranged a bedroll under her injured leg to prop it up, then rolled over on her side which seemed to be Troy's signal. He laid down on the blankets, turned on his side and moved very closely to Rachel's back, pulled a blanket over them, then draped his arm possessively around her waist.

When Pops was able to close his jaw and turned to Michael, he just dropped it open again when he saw the look on his son's face. Pops reminded himself right then and there to never doubt Mama again.

* * * *

It had been almost three months since Rachel's band moved into the village that warm April night. It was incredibly hot tonight. The temperature had reached over a hundred degrees during the day. Michael supposed that meant summer was here to stay for a while, if any season was predictable in these strange times. Just two weeks earlier, in late May, the temperature had dropped to 10 degrees requiring every adult in the village, including Rachel's band, to man the fire barrels and generators in the fields and the greenhouses all night. The cold snap had caught them off guard, maybe because they were getting a little too complacent. But it had kept Rachel there a few more days, so it had been worth something.

Michael still couldn't believe they were gone. Sarah had told them two weeks ago that Rachel and Troy had decided to move on, but she hadn't known exactly when they'd leave.

Sarah had cried for hours sitting in Mama's protective arms in their living room. If Michael had been honest, he would have admitted he felt like crying, too.

He had come out on the porch this morning to stretch and take a look at the new day and they had been gone. He hadn't even heard them leave. No goodbyes, no "I'll stop this way again sometime," no "I really enjoyed knowing you." Not even "I really do love you but I can't possibly do anything about it."

Michael shook himself from his melancholy. He and Rachel had kept their distance ever since that day in the greenhouse. He had spent a lot of time with the beautiful platinum-haired Karyn, and Rachel had spent every night in Troy's arms. He was amazed that they had survived together inside the same gates. He, Adam, and Pops had almost come to blows with Troy, Daniel and Joe. William had been off in the animal barn where he spent most of his time tenderly caring for the animals.

Rachel had effectively squelched the ensuing fight with one sentence, "When you boys are all done, I'll come and clean up the pieces 'fore any of the women see it."

Michael smiled sadly and ran the wet cloth across his face again, trying for some measure of relief against the heat. He thought back to that first Saturday that he and Mama had gone over to invite Rachel and her band to church the next day. Rachel had been forming her semi-polite refusal as Michael had known she would, when Karyn had joined them. Karyn had looked at Michael in that special way that always let him know she was his for the asking, "I came to see if you want to sing a duet with me in church tomorrow, and to remind you of the picnic today."

Mama had told Karyn that they had just come to invite Rachel and her family to church tomorrow. Karyn had not been able to mask the repulsive thought of having them in their chapel, but she had said, "Well, I hope you can make it."

Rachel had surprised them all by looking Karyn in the eye and saying, "I know better'n that, but we'll make it, jus' ta make Mama happy."

Rachel's whole band had come to church ten times alto-gether. Michael remembered every single time and exactly what they had been taught. He wrote it in his journal just to make sure. He requested the subject of chastity be taught. Twice. He wondered now if he had done that for himself or for Rachel.

Michael still could not believe she slept with Troy every night, it just didn't fit. It was odd how he had absolutely no problem controlling himself with Karyn. It was probably just because he knew she nor her family would stand for such behavior. That thought only made him feel worse for his behavior with Rachel. What kind of an example had he been for her?

Michael was able to smile again as he remembered Daniel and the others in church. He had never seen four more uncomfortable men than they were those first couple of Sundays, but Michael had to admit they did get a lot better. Sarah and Rachel looked right at home and were very intense listeners and great singers. Rachel wore her outfit she'd gotten for her birthday each time and always looked self conscious, but Michael thought she looked great.

He had talked to Sarah and William several times about the things they learned in church and why the earth seemed to be rebelling, because they were always curious and open. They finally talked to him about the girl, Ginny, that was hiding in the barn, but he had already known. He and Pops decided to just give them some time to work it out with Rachel before they made any decisions about her. William certainly had worked enough for both of them; the schedule was reduced by half while he was there. William was a hard worker and as strong as an ox. He had also been a natural with the animals and everybody seemed to like him.

Troy and Joe remained aloof and had barely spoken to anyone. Several people in the village complained about their eerie stares and said they didn't trust them. He and Pops decided to forget the incidents with Joe and the booby traps as long as it didn't happen again. Michael figured one of the band members had been at fault and Rachel confirmed his suspicions that day when she'd gotten all flustered and asked a lot of questions when he'd brought it up.

It happened again though, and he and Adam took Rachel aside and explained what had happened and that they thought Joe was responsible. It never happened again, but Joe had looked at Rachel with even more contempt after that. Everyone wondered why she let him stay with them when he so obviously disliked her. Michael was sure there was a lot more going on in that angry little man's head than anyone knew. He had seen Joe stare at Rachel with an ugly kind of desire when she hadn't been looking. It had given him the creeps and it was all he could do to keep from punching him for looking at Rachel like that.

Michael shook his head when he realized he was sitting on his front porch worrying about a far-away Rachel and what Joe might do to her someday when he got up enough courage.

Michael's mind shifted to Daniel. That was one embittered young man. He had taken to Michael right away, much to Rachel's chagrin. Michael actually enjoyed being around Daniel most of the time. He gave Michael respect, sometimes to the extreme just to rub it in with Rachel, and Daniel seemed to have a natural knack with the plants and had been a great help to Michael and Pops in the research lab helping them to solve some long-standing dilemmas. Daniel had even held some very intelligent religious discussions with him, but he had never lightened up when it came to giving Rachel the respect she deserved as his guardian.

Daniel's behavior toward Rachel was at least understandable, if not condoned, since she was the authority figure and most teenagers resented authority, but his behavior toward Sarah had everybody baffled. He was forever insulting her and picking on her. Ben had finally taken all he could stand one day and knocked Daniel out cold. Nobody said a word since everyone of them had wanted to do it themselves. They all liked Daniel, but when it came to being mean to sweet little Sarah, he didn't stand a chance. He was a lot better after that.

There were years of built up hurt and anger in Rachel's little mismatched family and Michael knew more than he cared to think about. He had never betrayed his promise of silence to Rachel about her father and mother, but it weighed heavily on his mind and he wished he could talk to Pops about it and ask for some advice on how to help them get over it.

A breeze finally began to stir about midnight. It found Michael still sitting on the porch, alternately worrying about Rachel and feeling so grateful for his own wonderful family and how he'd been raised. Logically, he would not even consider raising his own family any other way, which meant he would wed somebody like Karyn that could be the equal partner it would take to make that possible. He thought about Karyn and he could see her beautiful smile and could smell her vanilla perfume. She was smart and very devout in their faith. She had a good, strong family who got along great with his family.

He wasn't getting any younger and he desperately wanted his own children who looked like him and the woman he loved. He wanted to give Mama all the little grandchildren she craved and he wanted someone to hold during the lonely, cold nights. He wanted a family.

God help him, he wanted Rachel.

Last Fruits

Chapter 7

They were finally back. Rachel hadn't told any of them where they were going, so the last week of the month's journey had been pure hell. The weather was some of the foulest they had ever seen and even Troy was complaining about going north. She had pushed them hard and she knew they were exhausted, especially Sarah, since her injury had her out of shape. She herself was more weary than she had ever been, but they could rest for a while now.

Rachel looked at the remains that bore the marks of the fire. She was surprised that it still looked black after six years. It looked like the cellar was still intact. She would go down there tomorrow, in the bright light, and face her past. The old outhouse and barn were still standing and she was pleased to see the wellhouse was still in one piece.

Surprise settled over Rachel's face as she realized she had known some joy here. Certainly not from her family's situation, but from the raw beauty and majesty of the land. Memories of long stolen hours lying in the warm sunlight by the lake eased over her. She could almost feel the softness of the lush grass beneath her belly, the nearness of the abundant wildlife. The shared bounty she enjoyed with the deer, squirrel and rabbit made her mouth water—tart red berries, sweet yellow apples and musky nutmeats of every variety. She smiled as she realized these were her treasured childhood moments; nature's private gift to a lost and lonely child.

Troy came to her and stood silently, waiting to see what the only person in the world who had ever shown him any kindness wanted him to do. He had learned a lot about loyalty from those villagers. He wanted to be loyal to Rachel, he just hoped he had it in him. Finally Rachel spoke, "What do you think about stayin' here for a while, Troy?"

If he told her the truth, that he'd spent most of his life in this miserable north country and that he'd never cared to see it again, she'd be disappointed. It was clear she had just needed to get far away from that village and the man she could never have. He just didn't understand why it had to be north. Of course, she had pulled him from that snake pit a hundred miles south, so maybe she was from these parts.

Whatever the true reasons were, he'd remain by her side until he died if she'd let him. He knew it was probably the closest he'd ever get to being a member of a family. She was the only family he had, and Sarah and Daniel. He guessed William and that hidden girl of his were okay, too. He'd just as soon shoot Joe as look at him, but he'd wait for Rachel to give that order.

Troy answered as loyally as he knew how, "Looks fine to me. Reckon we'll get shot for trespassing?"

"Naw, I don't reckon. Let's set up in the barn, looks like it's gonna pour tonight," Rachel looked at the gray, rolling clouds and rubbed her leg that hurt twice as bad when it was going to rain. It was the last week in August and already the days were getting shorter, the regular days, anyway, that weren't ravaged with tornados, floods, acid rain, hail-balls the size of your fist or any other horrid thing that nature could toss out.

The old barn leaked in a dozen places, but it kept most of the rain and wind out. Joe disappeared and reappeared with two squirrels. It was Sarah's turn to cook, so the food turned out good. Everybody was so tired that they only lasted about ten minutes after the cleanup was finished and they had completed their inspection of the old barn. It was obvious that many a traveler had found shelter there, each leaving his own mark behind.

Trash had been the most common item left behind, but others infinitely more grateful for their shelter had left messages on the walls or little treasures of food for the next weary traveler to enjoy. William found two large cans of peaches that had turned their simple fare into a feast. No one said a word when William put two squirrel legs that just happened to be left on his plate into one of the peach cans that had his share of peaches in it and went outside. He still hadn't come back when everyone else was bedding down for the night, so Troy didn't bother assigning watch.

William came bursting into the barn about midnight, the fierce wind filling the entryway with mounds of fleecy white snow. He had two other people with him and was saying he'd never seen anything like it, explaining that he had to come in because the snow was burying everything alive.

Troy and Rachel were on their feet and in a defensive mode before William finished his first sentence. They looked at the small figure and then looked away, unconcerned, until they noticed the second, much larger figure covered with snow, making him look like a huge snowman. They asked William at the same time, "Who's that?"

"Oh! This here's Peter. We've been outside talking for hours. He's a missionary and was just gettin' out of the rain under our...my...." William looked at Joe warily before continuing, "Well, anyhow, the snow just came all at once like it was dumped from the sky. Messed up our good conversation, didn't it, Peter?"

Rachel was in a particular daze that only comes when you're snatched out of a deep, exhausted sleep much too soon. She was trying to grasp the situation and decide what to do. She didn't miss the real reason why William had never brought Ginny forward—Joe. She had often wondered why he persisted with his game that had to be costing him a lot of sleep. She had already made up her mind to let the girl stay if she was still with them when they reached this place.

Ginny was the least of her worries right now. The big man had come out from under his thin rain gear and was extending his cold hand toward Rachel. "Hi, Rachel, I am Peter. I understand you've met my family. I'm Naomi's fiance."

Rachel stood in shock as the information sank in. William began to smile, "Ain't it somethin'? I've been fillin' him in on all the goings-on in the village for the last months."

Peter added, "You cannot imagine how welcome this has been for me. I couldn't believe I found William and Ginny just sitting out here in the middle of nowhere, and to hear them talking about Naomi and all the people I love has brought me closer to home than I've been in a long time. I'll be heading that way next week, if I can find the courage to make that journey alone. My companion was killed.... It's been two years since I left Rocktown Village. A very long two years."

Daniel and Sarah heard what was going on, shrugged out of their blankets, and gave Peter a friendly welcome. Rachel marveled at how they had changed from the quiet, sullen teenagers they had been before their time in the village. She also noticed that Joe was awake, sulking over in the corner by himself. Some things just didn't change.

Rachel couldn't believe her fate. Without a second thought she grabbed a blanket around her shoulders, handed Peter one and asked Troy to build a fire inside the fire barrel. She looked at Peter with more sincerity and hope than she realized she had in her. "Peter, I know it's late, but will you teach us the villagers' beliefs—all of them?"

It took Peter a minute to realize what she was asking, then he smiled, already feeling a great kinship and warmth for this little group of people. "That's what I do, Rachel. I've been looking for you...well, for whoever it is that needed me here, so I'd be honored. You want to start now?"

Again Rachel didn't hesitate, "Yeah, right now."

Everyone looked at her in surprise, but not one of them went back to their beds. She looked over at Joe and invited, "Joe?"

"I didn't want to come to this God-forsaken Minnesota, and I shore ain't gonna get up in the middle of the night and listen to some stranger learn me things I ain't invitin'."

Rachel looked away before he could see her disappointment. Then she realized what he had just said. Minnesota. How did Joe know that? She hadn't told any of them that they would be in LeSueur County, Minnesota when their journey ended. She had gotten lost twice coming here, and they couldn't see more than inches in front of their faces for days sometimes, so she instinctively knew not one of them had figured out their destination, so how did Joe know where they were? They had not passed one sign, those had all been torn down long ago by angry mobs, and Joe hadn't wandered into their camp all those years ago until they had already traveled two weeks. None of them had ever talked about where they were from or what their families had been like. Rachel guessed their past had been just as rotten as hers, so who wanted to talk about that?

When Rachel's eyes met Sarah's, both sets were full of questions. Sarah had been having the oddest feelings about this place ever since they arrived, like she had been here many times before. Sarah hadn't missed that Joe said they were in Minnesota. The book she carried with her told her that they had been born in the Appalachian Mountains of Virginia. She had had little opportunity to learn geography, but she knew enough to realize those two places were in opposite directions. Sarah did recall moving once when she was very young, going on a long journey. As she began to remember other horrible things about that journey and the equally horrible things that happened once they'd reached their destination, she forced herself back into that hiding place that offered her peace and escape.

Rachel watched the emotions crossing Sarah's face and comprehended a truth that she had never suspected; Sarah didn't remember. That's why she'd let Ben into her heart and why she had been able to accept the villager's love for her without the caution she should have had from her experiences. Rachel sighed and questioned what she was about to do. Would she just be setting them all up for failure? Could they ever be the kind of people the villagers were? Could they ever really escape their horrid pasts and be something different, be *accepted* as something different?

Just as Rachel was about to give up, to accept what she'd been dealt and go back to that place that at least offered safety from more heartbreak, Peter spoke.

Never had Peter felt his adversary more strongly than he did at this moment. He had spent two miserable years trying to teach a people who were unteachable, trying to preach eternity when no one was willing to take control over his physical appetites for the few minutes it would take to plant the tiny seed of hope. He had been buried in a mudslide, broken in vicious winds that whirled trees at him, frozen in ice when the day before had produced such heat it had drained his body of all fluid, beaten and robbed so many times he had lost count, and just this night had been entombed in snow in the summertime.

It came to him in vivid force that the constant hunger, the acid wetness and the never-ending suffering of mankind wasn't going to end, that he was wasting his time and should go back to his comfortable life in the village. He mumbled to himself, "You'd really like me to believe that, wouldn't you? Then you could win and these people would be lost."

Somehow Rachel understood that Peter was dealing with the same heavy blackness that was smothering her, threatening to engulf her, body and soul. Her eyes reached out to him in a silent plea for something that she did not understand, could barely comprehend.

Peter reached over, took Rachel's hands in his and looked straight into her soul, "Wait here, please, for just a few more minutes." Peter started to rise and was slammed to the ground by some unseen force. It seemed to take all of his strength, and courage, to rise. He headed for the barn doors, but never made it outside. He dropped to his knees and his head fell to the ground in front of him. His hands clutched the dirt and straw at his sides.

Sarah began to sob and Ginny soon followed. The men looked to Rachel for guidance, asking with their eyes how to attack an unseen enemy. The confusion and hopelessness was tangible.

Just when Rachel was ready to concede, to forget she had ever felt that small light of hope, to release Peter from his burden, Peter straightened to his knees and bowed his head. He spoke aloud those words that could heal broken spirits and impart hope to those who would give place to his words.

When he was finished, the wind ceased its howling, the sky closed its windows and the moon and stars shone brightly through the cracks in the barn. After a time, Peter rose to his feet and once again took his position in their circle.

They waited for him to brag, to speak of his powers. He said, simply, "We can begin now."

* * * *

It was Monday, the sixth day of October and Naomi was inconsolable. Peter was supposed to have been home weeks ago and there had been no news. She had gotten ten letters altogether during the two years since he'd been gone, and seven of those had come the first year. The last one had arrived in June with a carrier who had demanded so much for his precious payload that Pops had almost refused him, but he'd made the mistake of looking into his daughter's eyes and had known at that moment he would have done anything to appease the yearning and sadness he saw there.

Peter's first line had been an apology for the carrier and the advantage he had known he would take, but he said he had weighed that against the anxiety he knew his family and Naomi would experience if he didn't get word of his well-being to them soon. It had been obvious that Peter had tried to temper his discouragement and the truth of his dire conditions, but everyone had been able to read between the lines. The village had mourned for weeks over the news that Peter's companion, also a son of one of the village families, had been beaten to death by a mob the first week in June.

Peter's one line that followed had been the basis for many sleepless nights for Naomi, "I nearly met with the same fate, but I am recovering."

For weeks Naomi and Christina, with Mama's advice here and there, had gone right on working on the wedding for October sixth at midnight. The tension had built until it was tangible.

"Ben! You are such an idiot! That flower goes over there," Naomi screamed from the other side of room.

"Okay, that does it! You're on your own, I'm out of here," Ben spat, and added over his shoulder as he walked out, "I have better things to do than stay here and get yelled at by a madwoman."

"Go ahead and leave! I don't need you, anyway," screamed Naomi.

Christina looked around for somebody who had the nerves for the screaming that Jeremiah was sure to perform when she handed him over. She needed to talk to Naomi, alone. Oh, how she missed Rachel. Rachel had nagged Jeremiah almost as much as she had during the months she'd been there, and it had been heaven. Her back had even stopped hurting. She eyed Michael as she stretched her aching back. He smiled and held out his arms, accepting the clinging baby boy who started wailing immediately. Michael covered the ear closest to Jeremiah with his free hand and headed for the door.

She wasn't really sure what she was going to say, so Christina just walked over to Naomi where she was busy slamming things around. Christina took Naomi gently by the shoulders and turned her around until she was facing her. Christina pulled her into her arms and soothed, "I'm so sorry, honey. Maybe we should just let things rest until Peter manages to get home."

Naomi pushed away and turned from Christina and shouted, "I will not stop! He will be here!" She turned back around and fell into Christina arms again, sobbing this time. "Oh, Christina, he has to be okay. He just has to be."

"I know. He has to be," Christina said. "He will be here soon, honey, I just know it. Okay?"

Naomi looked at Christina through her tears, nodding, "Okay. I love you, Christina, for sticking with me."

"Oh, sweetie, I love you, too, and Peter is a lucky guy. Just keep your chin up, deal?"

Naomi nodded again, blew her nose, then went right back to work on the last minute things for her wedding that was scheduled in exactly two hours, a special midnight ceremony, so the group of people, which included Adam, would be back from the church's semi-annual conference. Everyone was beginning to fear it was a wedding that probably wasn't going to happen.

Naomi stopped suddenly and said, "I need to apologize to Ben. I'll go find him."

Christina quickly offered, "I'll go. You go on over to the house and get freshened up and I'll be there in a few minutes to help you get dressed. I need to rescue Michael from Jeremiah anyway." She headed for the door, sure she was preventing another round between Naomi and Ben. Naomi was just too emotional to be reasonable with anyone right now. She looked around as she was leaving and noticed the room that had bustled with people earlier was empty except for Naomi. She would probably have jumped ship, too, if she hadn't been so conditioned emotionally by her clinging, petulant baby Jeremiah.

When Christina walked into Mama and Pops's normally calm, peaceful house, she nearly turned around and walked back out. Jeremiah was screaming at the top of his lungs back in the bedroom, Mama was sitting in the corner crying, unconsciously hugging her aching shoulder as had become her habit after the arrow, and Ben was sitting in a angry heap on the sofa. Pops peered cautiously from his bedroom doorway to see who had come in.

Christina decided to take care of the loudest problem first. She almost ran to Michael's bedroom to take Jeremiah in her arms. He quieted immediately, but continued to whimper softly against her shoulder, twisting her beautiful, red hair in his chubby little fingers.

His enormous chocolate-brown eyes looked into his mommy's and she caressed his little tawny head and thought once again what an exquisitely beautiful child this was who looked nothing like her. Jeremiah and Ben were the only ones who looked completely like Mama's side of the family, so it was funny how Jeremiah's eyes had taken on the exact sparkle and coloring as Michael's, since he was the only one who had Mama's eyes and everything else from Pops. She had often thought that particular mixture of light brown eyes with dark skin and hair was what served to make Michael so extraordinarily handsome.

Christina finally realized why Rachel loved to look at Jeremiah's eyes. She had caught them just sitting and staring comfortably into each other's eyes many times. She couldn't help but turn from her son's eyes to inspect Michael's. They were indeed the same.

Michael shrugged once Christina turned back to him, "I tried everything. Nothing works with him. He just doesn't want anyone but you...or Rachel."

The sadness in his eyes made Christina flinch. "Jeremiah is the least of our problems, did you see Pops hiding in his room? Mama is crying and Ben's steaming. They haven't even started dressing—and you saw Naomi's condition." Christina spoke again after some thought, "I hope Adam makes it back from the conference. We need him here. And where is Peter? What are we going to do, Michael?"

"I don't know. Mama is still so sad over Sarah leaving,...and Rachel, too, I guess. She told me earlier today that she just couldn't deal with losing Peter. She won't even talk to Pops and that's got him upset—angry, actually." A sudden, forced grin spread across his face, "We could run away together! You want to?"

Christina slapped him on the shoulder and grinned. "Leave it to you to make light of a dark situation."

Michael turned serious just as quickly, "I just can't bring myself to give up on Peter making it in time for the wedding. I know he may not even be in control of his circumstances, but...."

Christina stopped him when he paused, "I know. I feel it, too. I have just been hesitant to say it forcefully in case I was wrong, but I did just say as much to Naomi, so let's go finish up."

"Okay. Shouldn't Adam be back by now?" Michael asked as they walked toward the living room.

"He promised he'd be back in time for the wedding, even if he had to leave early. That's all he would tell me."

Michael fretted, "I probably should have volunteered to go and let Adam stay here with you."

"Again! Come on, Michael. It was Adam's turn. We have to keep enough people here to run things. You and Pops have gone the last several times and, besides, you had to stay here to look after the crops in this foul weather. Don't you get crazy on me, too," Christina exclaimed, looking truly worried.

"Don't worry. If I'm nothing else in the world, I am dependable and predictable," Michael explained.

It seemed to Christina that Michael had said that as though he loathed those characteristics. "Since when is that a bad thing?" Christina asked softly, sensing Michael's deep melancholy.

Michael looked away and was silent for so long that Christina was about to ask the question again. Then he looked into Christina's wonderfully green, understanding eyes and finally gave voice to the truth he had hidden so well, even from himself, for the last two months. "Since Rachel."

"I thought Karyn...," Christina started hesitantly.

"No."

Christina knew a flat "no" when she heard one. "I see."

They were so engrossed in their conversation that they didn't realize they had walked into the living room. Everybody, including Pops who had ventured from the safety of his bedroom, was staring at them. Ben's look had become even more ugly. He was just angry enough to say what everyone else was thinking. "Well, Michael, welcome to the Rock Idiot Club. What are we supposed to do? Go hunt Sarah and Rachel down and take them for our wives and run into the woods and raise little heathens?"

Michael's expression became so sorrowful that Ben was immediately contrite. "Ah, man, I'm sorry...I didn't mean that...I...."

Michael spoke softy, "It's all right, Ben. Somebody needs to tell it like it is, knock some sense into my thick head."

"Yeah, well, how about if we just knock each other out? That way we'll both be out of our misery," Ben retorted.

The knock on the screen door was soft, the kind that makes you look, but you're not really sure you heard anything. Sarah opened the door a few inches and peered in. She was silent for a moment, then stuck one foot inside and asked, "What ya'll so quiet about?"

Ben jumped up so quickly that he turned the sofa over. He grinned awkwardly and asked, "Sarah, what are you.... What's going on?"

"We brung you somebody," she smiled. She reached outside the door, grabbed Peter by the arm and shoved him in while shouting, "Surprise!"

The room erupted. Pops fell over the upturned sofa getting to Peter, Jeremiah became frightened from all the commotion and started screaming, Ben grabbed Sarah and twirled her around, knocking a lamp over, and Mama, Michael and Christina all reached Peter at the same time and managed a group hug, nearly smothering Peter.

Christina was jumping up and down, bouncing Jeremiah around so vigorously that he bit his lip and started screaming yet again. Once he quieted she said, "I'm going to get Naomi!"

Peter reached out and grabbed her arm, "Wait. Don't tell her I'm here. Just encourage her to go to the chapel and wait. Tell her you just know I'll make it."

When Christina looked skeptical, Peter added, "I know it's been hard on her, but I really want to see her for the first time at the altar. Please, it means a lot to me. I'll explain later."

Adam walked up on the porch just in time to hear Christina say, "All right, Peter Williams, but you'd better know what you're doing! The ceremony is in one hour."

Adam had run into Peter's group a few miles outside the village, so he shouted over the noise through the screen door, "Is that woman giving you a hard time, Peter?"

Christina hugged Adam so hard that Jeremiah started wailing again, so she kissed her handsome husband and Peter and Sarah. She then excused herself to go put the baby to bed, comfort a distraught Naomi and make sure the twins and Jeremy hadn't killed the babysitter.

After Mama had hugged Peter and Sarah a half-dozen times, she asked Sarah, "How in the world did you run into Peter? Are Rachel and the others with you, too?"

Sarah answered in a tired, but excited voice, "Yep, they're right outside. Rachel's the one that said we'd better escort Peter back, or he'd never make it by hisself. We found him...he found us, in Minnesota, where he ended up by mistake."

Mama thought that over for a minute, then looked directly at Michael and said, "That's two of my loved ones Rachel has brought back to me when nobody else could have. She's a special woman, and there's some reason God keeps sending her back to us."

Peter chimed in, "I'll say! Wait until I tell you the whole story about her band. Every one of them has converted...well, except one, but Rachel's...."

Michael walked quickly out the back door, he didn't want to hear that they had all accepted the teachings from Peter except Rachel. He just couldn't bear to hear that right now. He knew he'd have to deal with it sooner or later, but right now he just wanted to see her. Not up close, but from a distance, so he could think about things logically and put his feelings into perspective.

He peered around the corner of the house just in time to see Jeremiah reach for Rachel. She raised him over her head and twirled him around in the air while looking up into his face, grinning. She asked, "How's my punkin been? I've missed those beautiful eyes."

Christina just shook her head when Jeremiah giggled out loud. As soon as Rachel deposited the baby on her hip, Christina gave Rachel the welcome she had only hoped for. She hugged her soundly, then pulled back and said, "Well, Rachel, you've done it again, honey. You've come bearing very precious gifts. Thank you for Peter. I want you to promise me right now that you are never leaving again. I need you...no, that is not the right word...I will die without you, so, promise, right now!"

Rachel laughed, then whispered something in Christina's ear that left her speechless for a full minute. She quietly took Jeremiah back and started walking toward her house, then turned around and said, "You're appreciated here, regardless. Welcome home, honey."

Michael longed to go out and give Rachel the same care-free welcome that Christina had just given her. Why couldn't he just see her as a friend, as someone who had cared enough to risk her life for Jeremy, and now for Peter? Why did his heart have to flutter and hurt at the very sight of her, with her stringy hair and dust-covered manly clothing? He looked a little closer and he was sure she was even skinnier than before.

The men began setting up camp under the large lean-to that had never been taken down. Adam and Pops had appeared and were shaking hands with each of the men. He heard Daniel ask where Michael was, so he decided he had better make his appearance now. Michael had every intention of going straight to Daniel, but as he approached Rachel, who was several feet closer to him than Daniel, he knew he couldn't do it. He knew it would hurt her if he just walked past her, so he decided to trust his instincts, something he'd been afraid to do where Rachel was concerned for some time.

Rachel envied the confident way Michael was walking over to her. She could already see the sparkle in his eyes. How could he be so calm when she felt like her life was hanging by a thread, one that this man could snip with a few ill-fated words. She couldn't believe she had let herself become so vulnerable. She held her breath as Michael took the last few steps that brought them face to face once again.

Michael leaned very close to Rachel's ear and whispered, "If you would be willing to give me the hello you know we both are craving, then I would be willing to promise I won't let anyone tie you up for doing it." He pulled back and grinned, waiting to see what his instincts would bring him.

Rachel could feel the smile tugging at the corner of her mouth, and she knew before she looked that everyone was staring at them to see what they would do, so when she looked up at Michael, she allowed something to come forth that she had kept suppressed her entire life. She threw her arms around his neck and held onto something infinitely beautiful. It just didn't matter that it could only last for a few seconds, it was hers for the taking and she intended to savor it for as long as he offered it.

Michael lifted her off the ground and held her so tightly that she could barely breathe. He let out a yell as he twirled around with her that was so loud it brought Christina to her window to see what was happening. Rachel added her voice to Michael's with her own brand of merriment and was pleased when she heard everybody around them add their voices and whistles until the noise was so loud it blended together to form one magnificent sound of homecoming.

Michael set Rachel down gently and kissed her on the cheek, but never pulled away when she turned her lips into his and savored the wondrous feeling for just a second before smacking out a loud kiss that allowed them to break away with laughter.

Daniel was there immediately to punch Michael in the chest with a good natured slug. Michael grabbed him in a head lock and feigned to ask him the question, but was looking directly at Rachel, "So, are you going to stay this time, or leave me when I'm not looking?"

Daniel smoothed his hair and grinned, "I'm yours for life!"

Michael continued until he had extended a hardy welcome to each of the other band members, including the pretty little oriental girl with William. She introduced herself as Ginny, then pulled Michael close and said, "You give good welcome back. I hope Rachel keep you. You good looker." After Ginny patted Michael on the head, he gave a loud hoot of laughter.

As Rachel walked past she looked at him suspiciously and asked, "What?"

Michael laughed again, then moved close to Rachel and whispered conspiratorially, "Ginny thinks you should keep me because I'm a looker and I know how to give a good welcome. Pretty funny, huh?"

Rachel paled, then could feel the red creeping up her neck. How could he be so kind one moment, then make fun of her so easily the next? She didn't think it was funny at all—she wanted nothing more than to keep him, but it was a joke to him. To hide her embarrassment she grabbed at the nearest thing to offer a diversion, and that happened to be Troy. "Let's sleep right here tonight, Troy. That all right with you?"

Troy just nodded and began putting the blankets down.

Rachel looked triumphantly at Michael, expecting to see the angry flicker that always entered his eyes when her sleeping arrangements with Troy came up, but was shocked to see the deep wound she had inflicted. Michael just turned and walked away, and to make his point, he didn't even look back when Daniel called after him.

Chapter 8

It was midnight and Naomi looked like an angel waiting at the front of the church in her simple, elegant white dress. Peter was standing outside the door waiting to make his entrance at just the right moment so they could proceed to the inner room and the altar. He gave one last nervous look around and was surprised to see Pops and a number of other people gathered under the big elm tree that shaded the entrance to the chapel. He had spent many pleasant times under that tree with Naomi before and after church services. He smiled when he thought of the more frequent, sweet kisses he had stolen there once they had committed to their marriage.

Peter sensed that something important was going on, so he gave a worried look toward Naomi where she stood patiently waiting, still unaware that he had arrived, then hurried to see what was happening. Mama, Pops, Adam, Michael and Ben stood in a line, each holding their exclusive wedding lamp that would serve as the only lighting during the special midnight ceremony. They were facing Rachel, Sarah, Daniel, William and Ginny.

It only took a moment for the reality to sink in. Rachel and the others couldn't come into the inner area called the temple. Sacred, eternal covenants would pass between him and Naomi, and only those who had lived worthily and taken the same covenants could enter and witness them. Peter looked from one group of five to the other, and saw the pain that each of the ten bore, and wished there were some way he could intercede, but knew he could not.

Mama looked at Pops and pleaded, "Isn't there some

way?" knowing in her heart it was a futile desire, but feeling compelled to ask nonetheless.

Pops shook his head sadly.

William ventured, "Ginny and me, we could share one of your lamps. Shucks, you won't even know we're there. It ain't like we'll be takin' up any of the light or anything...and we want to see how it's done...we been talkin' serious like ourselves 'bout such things...as marriage." His color had risen while he was speaking until his face was a deep shade of rose.

The silence was painful. William had misunderstood the whole reason why they couldn't go into the wedding. The young man serving as usher at the door had told Rachel and her group that he had no lamps with their names attached. It was, of course, because their names had not been on the temple list.

The lamps had been Naomi's idea and her special project that she had supervised for weeks. They were beautifully and individually hand made, and she had managed to get them approved to take into the temple because they provided the necessary lighting. Their real value, in this instance, was that they symbolized each attendee's worthiness to enter the temple, along with the little bit of oil each would need to make it through the marriage ceremony.

Daniel offered, "I could prob'ly round up five lights for us if you could give me a few minutes, Peter. I might have to borrow some oil, though." Daniel looked at Rachel, and for the first time in his life, he desperately wanted to do something to help her. She looked so sad and it was so unlike her to display her need to be included all over her face.

Sarah was the one who noticed Michael did not have his lamp, "Hey, Michael, where's yours?"

Michael looked down into his empty hands, remembering, and looked back toward the entrance. Karyn was still standing just outside the door holding both their lamps, waiting for him. Michael implored Sarah, and then Rachel with his eyes and said, "I'd gladly share mine if I could," he shrugged sadly, "But it doesn't work that way."

Sarah queried, "Why?"

Rachel answered for him. She looked sadly at Karyn standing in the entrance now, ready and worthy to go in with Michael, and said, "It's not something he can share with us, Sarah. Come on, let's go back to camp."

Sarah looked pitifully at Mama, then at Ben before turning to follow Rachel. She didn't see Ben start to follow her before Pops gently pulled him back.

Peter watched for a few moments as his friends walked away, realizing how deeply in debt he was to each of them for making the moment that awaited him possible. When he turned away from them and went to claim what he had worked and longed for since he was a child, what he had strived to be worthy of all his life, he knew a moment of pure sadness that they couldn't come into the ceremony with him. He vowed that he would begin tomorrow to assure they never had to experience being turned away again.

Michael stood rooted to the spot, yet he knew he had to go to her, had to tell her. When he moved to follow her, Pops did not stop him, but he motioned for Peter to wait just another minute.

His long strides caught up with her quickly and he turned Rachel to face him. Michael was sure his heart had relocated itself to his throat when he tried to speak. "Rachel, this is only a practice. Don't let it push you away, keep you from preparing for the real thing that is yet to come. Please, keep trying."

Rachel squeezed his hand before pushing it away, "I'll try, Michael."

He nodded and then ran back to join his family. He put his arm around Peter and said, "Tomorrow we have work to do, but tonight we will allow nothing to displace your joy. Let's go get your bride!"

Their minds slowly turned to Naomi and Peter after that, but the experience would forever be etched in the deep recesses of their hearts. They would always remember that moment when five faithful souls looked into the longing eyes of those five who were not prepared. It was such a deep hurt that it could only be endured in light of the fragile hope that it could change for tomorrow.

Tomorrow.

Rachel looked back one last time and felt a stab in the region of her heart when Peter disappeared into the church, finalizing that they were being left behind. She didn't like it that Michael had just walked in with Karyn, but somehow she knew what Peter had been trying to share with her was of much greater worth than the kisses she could steal from Michael. In that moment she realized it wasn't about Michael.

She admitted even as that thought was enlightening her mind, that she was grateful for what Michael had said. She would probably be running away again if he hadn't given her some hope. She wasn't exactly sure what he meant when he said this was just a practice, but it was something to hang onto while she was experiencing this terrible rejection.

The dismal mood was tangible by the time Rachel's band settled around the fire under the lean-to. They sat in silence for almost an hour before Rachel's thoughts began to drift. Rachel wondered if they felt as vulnerable as she did. She scanned their faces and saw it there in each of their eyes. She wondered if she had led them to the greatest thing that could ever have happened to them, or if being here would end up making their terrible aloneness more pronounced, more complete. She honestly didn't know, but she had decided to give the little seed that Peter had talked about a chance to grow.

Her eyes finally drifted to Joe. He was sullen and dark with a smirk on his face that clearly said, "I told you so." Poor Joe. Of all the people she had been unfortunate enough to know, he was the worst. It wasn't his actions. He knew his limits and he had never pushed her too far. However, that wasn't saying much, since her tolerance for nastiness was about a million times greater than Pops or Mama would ever consider putting up with. She wished at times that Joe would go too far so she could be rid of him.

Rachel continued to study Joe openly, ignoring the curious looks from the others and the growing hostility in Joe's face. No, it wasn't what he did, but what he didn't do that kept the mystery going. Why hadn't he acted on the obvious dislike he had for her and why in the world did he stay with them?

For that matter, why didn't she just make him leave? Was she afraid of him? She shook her head knowing that wasn't it. Everyone in the band had asked her to part his company at one time or another, so she knew she'd have their grit behind her. He wouldn't stand a chance against all of them. Something else made her keep him around, she'd realized that much after he stabbed Sarah and she still didn't make him leave.

It really wasn't his help with the food, though it was a wonderful convenience. She and William were excellent hunters and trappers and could easily fill in if he were gone, but Joe never asked them to share in the hunt. It was as though he wanted to keep his value high. She remembered the few times the others had come up with game or some other food, usually accidentally, and how Joe would sulk for days afterward.

Rachel had never seen him this quiet. She continued to study him and marveled that she didn't feel any anger. She only felt bad for him, that he was even more closed off than she was. She knew the depths of that loneliness and could barely conceive of someone's being worse than her own. She guessed she actually cared about him.

She shook her head again and smiled a sad little smile. She would never have admitted such a thing a few months ago. These villagers had really influenced her whether she liked it or not. The things that Peter had taught them still had her head spinning. Sometimes it was so easy to believe in an all-powerful creator, but sometimes it just seemed like a marvelous fairy tale spun out of necessity to relieve human suffering. A tale to give hope to the hopeless.

From her position beside Ginny and William, Sarah got up and cautiously walked toward Rachel, watching her the whole time as though she was unsure of what she was about to do. Sarah couldn't stand to see that forlorn and confused look on her sister's face for one more minute without sharing what she knew could ease the pain. Mama had shared it with her so many times and it was a miraculous medicine. Sarah eased down to her knees in front of Rachel and put both her arms around her neck, hugging her so fiercely that Rachel fell from the stump onto her knees.

The others watched in disbelief, waiting to see the reaction of their rock-hard leader to this very unacceptable show of weakness. Rachel found herself kneeling on the ground, cradled in an act of love and compassion that finally dissolved the rock in her heart. She slowly raised her arms and returned her sister's embrace, suddenly wanting to make up for all the lost years. It was only moments before they felt two other sets of arms encircle them, and they both looked above them and saw William and Ginny smiling down at them. They stood up and brought them into their circle.

Troy looked at Daniel and shrugged, "Ah, hell." Troy and Daniel got up at the same time and when they reached the circle, Rachel had already opened it for them. All six of them smiled awkwardly within the circle, but they knew, every last one of them knew, that something wonderful was happening.

That was how Peter found them, huddled together smiling at each other with a child-like fascination on their faces. It was beyond his wildest hopes that they would have softened so quickly, knowing the depths of their deprivation. William noticed him first and opened a big beefy arm to him. When Peter joined that circle, it felt as natural and right as what he had just entered into with Naomi. Peter looked around the circle and smiled at each one individually. When he had held Rachel's eyes for a few sweet moments, he inquired, "Naomi and I were just saying that this night is too beautiful to waste indoors, so we were wondering if you would mind if we held our reception out here with you?"

Sarah blurted, "But all the beautiful flowers and tables of food...."

Peter interrupted, "...are nothing compared to the beauty in this circle and the glory in the stars."

Rachel's face split into a full grin as she said, "Well, only if you bring the food out here, too!"

Peter broke from the circle and started running toward the chapel, calling back over his shoulder, "I'll get everybody and we'll be right back. Stoke up the fire!"

Within fifteen minutes there were tables of food and most of the village's people clamoring around, eating, singing and dancing in the street in front of their camp. A small band had assembled under their lean-to to help keep the dust out of their instruments. The first couple of songs were slow and boring, then Naomi asked them to play an oldie, "Tie A Yellow Ribbon 'Round The Old Oak Tree," in honor of Peter's return, and things picked up considerably after that.

Rachel stood with a shoulder leaned up against the big metal post that held the back of the lean-to in place, tapping her toe to the beat of the oldie the band was performing. She was marveling that this group of normally very serious people could be having so much fun and that not one of them seemed to mind that they had ended up outside in the dust with the flies. They were never very bad inside the village walls, but they nonetheless buzzed around demanding their share of the delicious food.

"A penny for your thoughts," Michael whispered in Rachel's ear.

Rachel started, "Good grief! Don't sneak up on people like that!"

"I didn't sneak, I just walked right up." Michael smiled. "It's just that you were so far away. Where were you, Rachel?"

"Somewheres out of the dust and away from these dang flies," she swatted at one that was trying to land on the piece of pie Michael had in his hand, then smiled happily up into his face.

Michael smiled back and said, "You look almost happy enough to dance with me."

Rachel thought about that for a minute, then asked, "You know how to polka?"

"I've done it once or twice," Michael lied.

"Well, I'm not very good at it," Rachel lied, "But I guess we could give it a shot."

Michael walked over to the band that was taking a quick break, and within minutes they struck up a fine polka song that brought half the village to the street. When Michael walked out with Rachel a path cleared and the village people stood back and waited for the treat they knew would follow any time Michael walked onto the dance floor.

He had served a mission in Poland and had learned to Polka from the masters during his personal days off each week. He asked Rachel to give him just a minute, knowing the village people would harass him until he performed for them. He moved out away from her and executed one of the finest renditions Rachel had ever seen.

Rachel had to smile at Michael's baffled expression when she asked him to give her just a minute once the next song had begun. Before the street could fill she launched into a performance that could only be classified as second to none. Michael hesitated for just a moment before he joined in clapping with everyone else and decided to enjoy the fact that he had just lost his status as the best polka dancer in the village.

* * * *

"...so you see, we want you and your family to have our house." The very old man and woman smiled at each other in a way that made Rachel yearn inside.

Rachel stared at them, dumbfounded. Words just wouldn't form in her mind. They wanted to give her their house? When her thoughts could finally form and verbalize, she was embarrassed that they revealed her selfish, cynical nature, "Why would you do that for my...my family?"

"Why child, because you are one of us now! You brought our Peter back to us. You are important to all of us, so you can't keep sleeping out here in the elements." Peter's grandmother looked at Rachel as though she had explained it all, then smiled conspiratorially, "It's the biggest house in the village. See, we have lived here our whole lives, long before the gathering, so we managed to keep our own house. We raised eight children and three grandchildren there. It has a wonderful spirit in it that will help you to grow, and raise your children, too." Grandmother Williams smiled and reached for Rachel, pulling her into a hug that only a grandmother could produce.

Once she could breathe again, so tight and wonderful had been their embrace, Rachel managed to say, "I couldn't take your home...."

Grandmother Williams interrupted her, "Nonsense! We're almost ninety years old, and we can't take care of that big boat any longer! We need your help. Peter and Naomi don't even want it, they'll be staying at our son's house, Peter's father. Now that they'll be there to liven the place up, we've decided to accept our son's invitation to live with them. He's been bugging us for years!"

Taking a deep, but frail, breath, Grandmother Williams continued, "Their house is almost as big as ours, so there's plenty of room. I think they're lonely. We'll just let the young ones worry about everything now, right Grampy?" The old man shook his feeble head in agreement and smiled at Rachel through bleary, aged eyes that revealed nothing but pure love for the woman who had cared enough to traverse hundreds of miles to bring their favorite, beloved grandson home safely to them.

There weren't any words of gratitude good enough for what this elderly man and woman had just done for Rachel and her family. They were offering them a real home and all the love and friendship they had never known. Rachel just stood there, speechless.

Grampy spoke quietly, "Well, it's all decided then. The Council has already approved it, we asked before we came to you just to make sure it was all right, so you can move in tomorrow. It may take us a few days to get our personal belongings together, but we want your family to have everything else."

Michael walked up just as Grampy finished his sentence and said, "Grandmother and Grandfather Williams! It's two o'clock in the morning and you're still dancing?" Michael gave them one of those smiles that made Rachel's stomach do flip-flops even though she hadn't been the recipient of it.

Grandmother spoke for them, "We're finished, I tell you. Bamboozled, fried, gone! Will you and Rachel walk us home so we can put these old bones to bed? That way we can show Rachel her new home."

"So, you've told her!" Michael looked into Rachel's eyes and gave her one of those grins that transforms space and time. "Well?"

Rachel shifted uncomfortably as all three of them watched her intently, waiting for her reaction to their unbelievable generosity. Tomorrow she would die of humiliation when she had time to think about her behavior, but nothing could have stopped the tears that flowed freely down her cheeks, while she choked out the words, "Thank you."

Michael put a protective arm around Rachel's shoulders, effectively concealing the emotional state that was disgracing this proud woman. Then he announced to the two elderly people who had nodded appreciatively after Rachel's thank you, "We'd be happy to walk you home." Michael motioned for them to lead the way.

Rachel had only vague impressions of their walk across the village to the beautiful old victorian home that sat in the far western corner by the small playground and park. Rachel could see immediately in the bright moonlight that the house had a fresh coat of snow-white paint and that the fine victorian detail was trimmed in the very lightest pink. The porch that completely surrounded the house didn't even creak when they stepped onto it. It sprouted a dozen or more lattice-backed rockers and large hanging plants hung from every post above the railing.

Grampy motioned toward the rockers and explained, "At first we only had two rockers, then we added one for every child we had. We've replaced and repaired them over the years so the children still have theirs when they come to visit. The others have been added by neighbors just because they like to sit and visit after church on Sundays and the others were always full." He chuckled and continued, "I can't promise you they'll stop coming, it's tradition."

Grandmother Williams added, "I give each flower a dipperful of water everyday, they seem to like it better that way. I'll leave the porch lamp burning for now, but you'll need to put it out when you leave." She opened the screen door that looked as though new screen had just been put in and motioned for Rachel and Michael to come in.

Rachel's breath caught as she entered the long, wide hallway with beautiful old lamps, decorative wool rugs and a scrolled table with a flat back against the wall. It held generations of pictures. To the left was a huge living room and to the right was the stairs leading to the upper two stories and attic. The staircase was so polished it glimmered in the lamplight and the thick runner was held in place by a brass rod at the base of each step.

Further to the right was a kitchen that was almost as big as Michael's house. It had a massive wooden picnic style table made of oak, with benches along the sides and a chair at either end that Grandmother Williams proudly announced could seat twenty people. There were copper pots and utensils hanging over the huge stove that looked like they could hold enough food for an army. An antique china cabinet held plain, but beautiful, heavy white ceramic dishes with little pink roses painted around the edges. The floor had real ceramic tiles that were pale beige with the same light pink roses in them. A large rag rug with alternate rings of the very lightest pink and white lay clean and fresh under the big oak table. Large potted plants were crowded into the bay window that had its twin on the other side of the house in the living room.

Grampy grabbed Rachel by the arm when she stood mute in the middle of the kitchen, and dragged her across the hall into the living room, "This is the best room, Rachel, my favorite. Even when we're alone, we feel like all our children are here with us."

It didn't take Rachel long to figure out why Grampy had said that. The huge room made you feel like you were jumping onto a fantastic plush pillow when you entered its doorway. There were crocheted afghans, homemade quilts, tons of embroidered pillows, and thick, wool rugs of every color and size imaginable, all of which seemed to come together in a perfect symmetry of color.

The massive collection of family pictures was the prominent eye-catcher for Rachel. They sat in beautiful old frames on every table, they filled the top of the handsome old piano, they hung on every wall. The biggest was a painting of Grandfather and Grandmother Williams with all eight children, including their spouses and children, hanging over the mammoth fireplace which covered nearly a whole wall.

Rachel stared at the stunning colors and the figures that were so life-like their eyes looked as though they'd blink at any moment. She found herself counting the people and whistled when she counted the last. Forty-two people!

Grampy chuckled and said, "You should have been here, Rachel. It took the artist two weeks to complete that painting. Twenty-two sittings in all, plus his work on the side from photographs. The women had insisted it had to be live. Oh, were these old floors hopping with activity during that time! We had forty-four souls stuffed in here for the better part of three weeks." Grampy clapped his hands and laughed harder this time. "You've never encountered a more sour group by the time we gathered in the same clothes for those last few sittings."

He pointed to a Peter of about ten years old and another

grandson, then looked sheepishly at Grandmother as he told the story. "These two grandsons, you know Peter, and this one is Joseph, were so bored and resentful by the last sitting that they brought ants and turned them loose on the girls!" Grampy laughed and Grandmother scowled.

Grandmother fumed, "I still fail to see what you find so humorous about that whole thing. Our granddaughters had welts for a month and we had mostly quarreling among the children after that!"

Rachel was almost sure she saw a grin tugging at the corner of Grandmother William's mouth. She looked at Michael who was grinning widely, realized this was probably a standard routine for the older couple and began to relax a little.

After another half-hour of touring, Rachel and Michael bid them good night, blowing out their porch lamp as they departed. As they were slowly walking back toward his house and her camp, Rachel broke the silence, "Is this real, Michael?"

"Yep."

Rachel was silent for a few more moments, then smiled, "Did you count the bedrooms?"

Michael grinned, fully enjoying Rachel's awe, "No. How many?"

"I can't believe it! Counting those two little biddy ones in the attic, there are ten, and I counted four bathrooms! Shew! I ain't never even had one *inside* before." Rachel looked away with embarrassment when Michael's grin faded away and was replaced with sympathy.

Michael knew they needed a subject change or that look that just came over Rachel would leave them arguing again. He couldn't think of anything to say and was surprised as he watched her get her pride under control so quickly. He knew it was probably a mistake, but couldn't help pointing out, "With all of those bedrooms you can finally have some privacy."

Rachel knew he was talking about Troy and decided it

was time to explain some things. She had wanted to explain the last time she was here, but had enjoyed Michael's displays of jealousy too much to give them up. It was funny how differently someone could come to think about something in such a short period of time.

Peter had taught them so much about honesty and fairness, that she had realized something very important. If she were ever lucky enough to capture a good man's attentions, she wanted it to be based on truth and respect, not something like jealously or lust.

Taking Michael's hand, Rachel guided them over to the little park and took a seat on one of the swings. Michael offered, "Want a push?"

She smiled, but shook her head. "No, I want to talk. Really talk...without getting angry. Being prideful is what Peter would call it. Do you think we can do that, Michael?"

Michael sat in the swing next to Rachel and looked deeply into her eyes, "I'm sure of it, Rach."

Rachel groaned inwardly at the endearment. She honestly did not want those strong emotions that turned her inside out every time she was around Michael. She wanted to be able to talk to him like she talked to Peter or William. There was no point in denying it though. She longed for this man, only Michael, to take her in his arms and swear eternal love to her, but she also knew she wanted it the way Peter and Naomi had it. She wanted the sweetness and rightness that was shared between Pops and Mama, or Adam and Christina.

It was far too much to expect and she feared she could never have it. She knew just as well that she would regret it the rest of her life if she couldn't have it. She knew the difference now; how could she ever go back to not knowing?

Peter had assured all of them, over and over again, that the happiness and peace the villagers had was possible for anyone. He had said it was possible for them, with enough effort. Though she tried not to, even feeling petty because she did, Rachel looked at Michael and knew that he was the only one that could ever fully fill this new void in her life. She knew just as well that she could never have him.

After several moments of silence, Rachel finally summoned the courage to just spit it out, "Look, Michael, there is nothing going on between me and Troy. I have never done...that with any man. He just acts like we do so others will leave me alone. He thinks he's protecting me. He started sleeping beside me several years ago when two men were camped with us and one of them kept staring at me until everybody in camp got the creeps. He backed off and left after Troy made his show of claiming me."

"But even Sarah thinks it's true," Michael whispered with all the pent-up anxiety that he'd harbored for months over this very thing. A spark of hope began to build where only pain had been.

"I know. It hurts me that Sarah and Daniel had to believe it, but Troy thinks it keeps Joe in line, too, so we couldn't tell them. It's too hard to keep a secret like that when you're young as they are. Troy was afraid Joe would find out and then he'd have to kill him over me. I didn't want that to happen, for some reason I don't understand." Rachel shrugged and fell silent again.

Michael asked, "Rachel, why do you let Joe stay?"

"Honestly, I don't know. Maybe 'cause he's so sad. I guess he ain't got nobody else to be sad with." Rachel looked away in shame, then added, "Besides, Peter says it's a sin to turn the needy away."

Finally finding the courage to ask the question he'd been avoiding since their arrival, Michael queried, "I overheard Peter saying one of you wouldn't accept his teachings...."

"And you knew it was me." Rachel looked into his eyes and saw the truth of her words. "Come on, we'd better get back. Christina said she needed me to tote Jeremiah." The smile that Rachel attempted came far short of reaching her eyes.

Michael sighed and nodded his head, wishing he had never asked the question. He could have at least had one night of hope, although it would have been false hope. Why was he doing this to himself? He knew it could never work between him and Rachel. He loved the gospel and his family's way of life more than anything, and he knew he would never give it up for any woman. He had just hoped something, some miracle might....

"It was Joe," Rachel stated.

"What?"

"I was the first one baptized, but Joe wouldn't even listen to Peter," Rachel held her breath, waiting.

Michael let that sink in for a minute, then he couldn't prevent the face-splitting grin that spread across his features.

When Rachel finally breathed again, she returned his grin in like measure. She wasn't prepared when Michael grabbed her off her feet and drew her up into a bear hug. When he set her down, she asked, "What was that for?"

"For everything, Rachel. For being you. For teaching me."

Rachel looked incredulous, "What could I teach you?"

"That I should practice what I preach, but I don't quite have it yet. Will you keep teaching me?" Michael had gone to a slightly teasing mode, so he was grinning mischievously.

"It's a tough job." Rachel retorted.

The walk back to the festivities was silent, each lost in their own wondering, but halfway back Michael reached down and took Rachel's hand possessively in his.

Chapter 9
Two Months Later—Mid December

"No!" Rachel looked at the startled faces surrounding her, their bafflement only fueling her anger. How could they not know what they were doing to her. "NO! Sarah, I will not help you put up a Christmas tree today, NO! Daniel, I will not make you some brownies, NO! William, I do not approve of you and Ginny having a Christmas wedding, and NO! Amy and Paul, you cannot spend the night again. Go home. Now!"

The twins looked at each other and shrugged, then headed for the door. Rachel tossed their pillows at them, Paul's hitting him in the back of the head. She started straightening the sofas where they had been sleeping just a few minutes earlier and didn't even notice Paul's reaction until he screamed, "Hey, I didn't do anything to deserve that! You're mean, Rachel!" He ran out the door sobbing.

Amy looked indignantly at Rachel and pouted, "He's right." She stomped to the door, then looked back at Rachel sadly and decided to close it softly.

Rachel slumped onto the sofa and rested her head on the back, expelling a long, frustrated sigh. She hadn't meant to hurt their feelings. She closed her eyes, refusing to look at the others, knowing she had probably hurt their feelings, too, so she did the one thing she had been longing to do for days; she got up, grabbed her coat and escaped to the barn.

Princess Mocha had just given birth to twin fillies yesterday. Rachel stood beside Michael's beautiful bay mare and stroked her silky-coarse mane. The babies had been lying peacefully, but the excitement of a visitor brought them quickly to their mama's side seeking her nourishment.

Rachel smiled when they both started tugging so fiercely, one on each side, that they had their mama's udder swinging from side to side.

Rachel knelt by the smallest one and positioned its head so she could get a good look at it. She giggled when it started licking her nose. She looked up at Princess Mocha's calm, contented countenance and envied her the comfort and joy she found in her role as mother. The horse lowered her head and gave Rachel a friendly nudge with her muzzle. Her large, soft eyes welcomed Rachel into her world and gave her a soft whinny to prove it.

Rachel couldn't believe she had become so attached to a horse, that she felt so comfortable and natural around her. "How do you stay so calm when they're tuggin' at you from both sides? It seems like you always know just what to do. When to fuss, when to just pay 'em no mind...."

"She's had some practice," Michael offered. He had both of his arms propped on top of the stall wall, looking down at Rachel where she sat indian style on the hay in the huge birthing stall. "Those two make ten babies altogether. Most horses can't deliver healthy twins, but it seems to be her specialty. You should have seen her with the first ones though. She had a nickname back then."

Rachel was annoyed at first that someone had intruded on her moment of solitude, but couldn't help warming to Michael's friendly smile. "Oh yeah? What was it?" Rachel asked with a genuine interest about her favorite horse.

"Dizzy Lizzy."

"Well, I don't believe it! Look at her, Michael. She's so calm she just might fall asleep—and she's not old, either." Rachel thought for a moment. "Lazy Lizzy, maybe."

Michael laughed, "No. I promise it was Dizzy Lizzy. She used to charge straight for you if you came within a hundred feet of her baby, and if you taunted her from over here, she'd ram or kick the wall. She hit her own head so hard one time that she was dizzy for a whole day. She staggered around like she was drunk. That's when she got her name."

Rachel laughed, trying to imagine sweet Princess Mocha in a tizzy. She looked at Michael and knew there was more.

"But what made her keep the nickname for so long was when she had her first twins the next year. They were rowdy little buggers and bounced all around this stall like ping-pong balls. Princess Mocha thought they had to be right by her side, touching her, to be safe, so she went in constant circles for days, frantically trying to control both of them at the same time." Michael stopped to laugh at the memory, slapping his knee like Rachel had seen Pops do so many times. "The more she went after them, the higher and faster they bounced!"

"Poor thing!" Rachel exclaimed. "She just didn't understand. Why didn't you do somethin'?"

"Me? What could I do? She was already in the safest place she could be, she just hadn't realized it yet."

Rachel looked so worried, "How long did it take her to get it all figured out? To get calm like this?"

Michael sensed that Rachel had more riding on his answer than how she felt about his prize mare. He knew she had been very tense lately. Maybe frustrated was a better word. He rolled it all around in his head and knew he shouldn't tell her it had taken Dizzy Lizzy three sets of twins to become Princess Mocha.

"Well, she's been Princess Mocha for a long time now. I haven't heard anyone call her Dizzy Lizzy in years. I suppose she barely remembers being that other horse." Michael was surprised to see the anger flash in Rachel's eyes after his answer.

"Don't sugar-coat it, Michael. How long?"

"Three sets of twins," Michael admitted.

"So, three years?" Rachel continued to quiz.

"Five. She had a single colt in between two of the sets of twins. She'd settle down with the one, then two would come along and set her off again." Michael had decided if she wanted it all, he'd give it to her, but he would much rather have been comforting her.

"Why, Michael?"

Michael knew what Rachel was asking, but pretended he didn't, to put off answering such a hard question. "Why what?"

"Why is life like that? Just when you get your breath, just when you think you can meet the day head-on, you get slapped in the face again."

"I guess it's all in how you look at it. You can either say those twins gave her the opportunity, the experience to become what she is now, or they were just rotten things that happened to her." Michael looked into Rachel's eyes and knew his answer was probably one she wasn't ready for yet.

Rachel looked away and sighed, "I see it as a rotten thing, so where does that leave me?"

"With the rest of us, I guess."

"I'm not like you, Michael. I'm not even sure I want to be like you."

It was Michael's turn to be unprepared. He stared at her questioningly, trying desperately not to be offended, but was nonetheless. He decided against responding at all, so he just stood there silently.

Rachel saw the hurt she'd just caused him, but was far beyond controlling her emotions, so she plunged forward, somehow knowing this man could deal with everything she threw at him. That made her more angry, because she was having so much trouble dealing with anything at all. "People like you are always trying to change anybody who's not like you. You think you have all the answers, and you make the rest of us feel like idiots. You have as many weaknesses as anybody else, but you cover it up with your ridiculous routines and traditions. Do you know I could set my clock by your run everyday? Do you have any idea how dumb you look runnin' 'round and 'round the village like that, and gettin' nowhere?"

"Why are you so angry, Rachel?"

She was about to go into another tirade when it dawned on her why she was saying such hateful things. She let out a long, angry breath and dropped her head into her hands. After the worst had passed, she stated, simply, "I'm angry at you because you're everythin' I'm afraid I'll never be able to be."

After long minutes, Michael whispered, "It takes a big person to say something like that. Maybe you'll be more than any of us."

"Do you know what I really want, Michael?"

"What, Rachel?"

"To feel like I deserve that wonderful old home I've been given. To feel like I can handle this chance to live like a real family. To feel like we'll be worth all the time and effort your people have given us." Rachel looked into Michael's steady brown eyes and finished with the one thing she feared to say the most. "And to feel like I could deserve someone like you."

Michael let that all sink in for a moment and asked, "Someone *like* me, Rachel, or *me*?"

"You, Michael."

"We could...." Michael started.

"We could what, Michael? We're as far apart as it gets here in this village. Peter tells me the end is near and there is very little time to prepare. I'm not prepared, Michael. I don't like getting up everyday and facing everything that has to be done to keep that beautiful old house beautiful. I don't like feeling like I have to read and pray and go to church all the time. I don't even like you."

"No one ever told you it would be easy." Michael stated flatly.

"Yeah, well, nobody ever told me I'd lay awake at night worrying about killin' the ferns that Grandmother Williams started when she was a child, and fearin' I'll forget and curse in church, or that I'll teach Christina's kids somethin' bad— and let's not forget I'm supposed to know what to do with William and Ginny, control Daniel, nurture sweet little Sarah and keep Troy and Joe from killin' each other inside the walls of that house!"

Michael spoke with similar passion, "Yes, I know what you mean. Nothing could have prepared me for these years of loneliness, and I'm so afraid I'm going to understand something all wrong and...." Michael suddenly realized what he was doing and fell silent.

Rachel's jaw dropped open. Well. Michael wasn't as perfect as he seemed. Suddenly she couldn't even remember what had been so important to her, what had her so upset just a moment ago. She was completely focused on Michael and this new side of him. "And what, Michael?" she coaxed quite sincerely.

Taken in by her concern and the need to share his burden, too, Michael surprised himself by continuing, "And mislead these good people, or get sick and not be able to do my part. A lot of people depend on me." Michael shrugged wearily. "Sometimes I want to shout at everyone and just tell them to leave me alone. I feel like I'm being smothered here, sometimes." He looked at Rachel sheepishly and fell silent once again, knowing he had everything in the world to be thankful for, already feeling sorry for having sounded so childish and selfish.

"Did you come out here to hide?" Rachel mused.

"That would be me." Michael gave a half smile.

"Well, I was here first, buster! But I have to admit, after listening to you, my problems don't seem so bad now." Rachel gave her own half-smile.

"I'm glad I could help you out." Michael teased as he kicked at the dust with the toe of his boot, but the smile never quite made it to his eyes. "I have to go, duty awaits. See you, Rachel."

Rachel wondered as she watched Michael leave the barn how two people could live in such close proximity, yet know so little about each other. She was going to have to do something about that.

* * * *

Rachel watched Michael as he headed down the street with a sack of something over his shoulder, just as she had been watching him ever since that morning in the barn. She had decided to perform a little experiment—a study actually. She was going to figure out what made Michael tick, what made him willing to run around in little circles and rush to complete his long list of rituals everyday, and, just maybe, she could learn something about her own unwillingness in the process.

Michael crossed the street and took the porch steps two at a time to the Peterson's, whistling all the way. Grandmother Williams came to the door, smiled a welcome, then opened the door to let Michael in. Why was Grandmother Williams at somebody else's house? Sarah came and sat in the rocker next to Rachel and asked, "What ya lookin' at?"

"Michael."

Sarah smiled, wondering how long it would take Rachel to realize what she'd just said. Of course she was looking at Michael. She'd been looking at Michael for a week now. Well, not really at Michael. Sarah had figured that out right away. It was more like she was studying what he was doing. "So what's Michael doin' now?"

"Don't know. Why is Grandmother Williams at the Peterson's?"

Sarah answered, "Mrs. Peterson has the sores, so Grandmother Williams is over there helping with her children."

Rachel looked at Sarah with the same frightened, shocked expression Sarah had had when she'd found that spot on her arm. "The village people have the sores?"

"We get them once in a while, but don't worry, they go away with the right care," Sarah explained.

"What do you mean *We* get them. You've had 'em?"

Rachel asked incredulously.

"Just one spot, but Mama fixed it right up, and Pops and Adam gave me a blessing."

Rachel demanded, "And why didn't I know anythin' about it?"

Sarah cringed at the anger in her sister's voice, but answered calmly, "It was back when your leg was hurt, so I didn't want to worry you."

After Rachel had been staring away angrily for several long minutes, Sarah ventured, "You reckon Michael is takin' 'em some food?"

Rachel never had the opportunity to answer since Michael came bounding out the door, then ran over to the porch where they sat with heavy sweaters on in the unusually warm weather and asked, "What are you two lovely ladies up to?"

Sarah answered timidly, "I'm just sittin' here. Makin' her mad. Again." Her words seemed to gather an edge about them as she spoke. Sarah looked at Rachel and decided to do something that would probably have Rachel giving her nasty looks for a week. "And Rachel's just sittin' here watchin' you."

Rachel's head jerked around and Sarah cringed again. Michael looked at Rachel's angry expression and blurted, "What have I done now!"

Sarah got up and headed for the door with an angry expression on her face now. She retorted over her shoulder, "Probably nothin', Michael, but that won't stop her from screamin' at you!"

Michael just stood there for a minute while Rachel stared off into space, watching her emotions go from anger to sadness. Finally he ventured, "Want to talk about it?"

Rachel surprised herself by realizing she certainly did want to talk to him. "Yeah. You have time to sit for a while?"

Michael knew that he was so far behind now that it would take him until midnight to get caught up, but he answered, "Of course I have time for my favorite lady."

Michael's lighthearted treatment of something that had

become so important to Rachel set her off again. She spat, "Michael! I am not your favorite lady, so why do you say that to me? Just save it for one of these village girls that follow you around like you're their knight in shinin' armor, just prayin' you'll come and rescue them."

Michael sat heavily into the rocker Sarah had just left and wished he had never stopped to say hello. Rachel was obviously in one of her foul moods. "You're right, Rachel, I am too frivolous with my speech at times. I'm sorry."

Rachel decided to press on since she really didn't want to talk about him right now. "Why didn't anyone tell me Sarah had the sores?"

"I don't know. I didn't know she had them either. Why?" Michael asked.

"Why! That is a death sentence out there, Michael. How can everybody be so calm 'bout it? Is it so different inside these walls?" Rachel challenged.

"Yes."

When Michael said no more, Rachel realized he wasn't going to talk to her until she calmed down, so she did the one thing she had become sick to death of doing; she conformed. In a much quieter, calmer voice, she asked, "What's really goin' on here, Michael? How did this all happen, this village, where did it begin? Why do we drink pure water and treat leprosy like it's a flea bite when the rest of the world's dyin' out there? Why, Michael? How?"

Michael knew it was time. He felt it deep in his stomach, that feeling you get when you're certain of something and it can't be denied. He had wondered how long it would be before Rachel realized how much more there really was to know, before she realized how hard it was to keep doing what was right. He wondered with a sad pang in the pit of his stomach if she would do it, if she would be willing to go over those hard miles that would bring her to true safety. Everlasting safety.

"Michael?"

Looking straight into her eyes he began, "Rachel, I'm

not speaking to you as a friend...or as someone with a special interest in you as a woman, though I am certainly both of those things. I am speaking to you as an authority in the Church." When Michael saw the flick of anger and challenge rise in Rachel's eyes, he knew he had to get this point across before he could do justice to what he was trying to explain.

He plunged ahead, "I'm explaining this so you'll receive what I'm saying in the same way you received and accepted what Peter has taught you. I know I'm not a missionary, and I know I've been less than a good example for you, but I have been called of God, Rachel. I love Him and it has become my opportunity to fill in some holes for you about how He works among his children who are true to him. Do you understand what I'm trying to say?" Michael's eyes pleaded with Rachel, and in their depths could not be found one ounce of vanity or pride, only humility.

Rachel did understand. She acknowledged in her own way by asking, "Were you a missionary, Michael?"

"For two years, three months, and twenty-one days."

"I bet you were a good one."

With that simple acceptance of his authority, Michael nodded and began the most important sermon of his life. He had given many in his short years, had been told by scores of people that he was the best speaker they'd ever encountered, but it was with utter humility that he began this one. Never had he been called upon to teach such an important aspect of his beliefs to someone he had a romantic interest in, and he realized an important test loomed before him. He realized in that single moment in time just before he spoke that it wasn't these good people of the village he had been so afraid of misleading. It was Rachel. Before him lay the eternal question: Whom do ye love and serve?

There was nothing to do but go straight to the heart, so Michael began, "The members of the Church in our country were being prepared for years against the time when we would need to gather again. Some other Christian groups were working hard to get their members ready, too."

Michael's voice was a little shaky, but he spoke with certainty and his eyes never wavered from Rachel's. When she nodded and urged him on with the acceptance in her eyes, he continued, "But it is hard to stay prepared, to watch constantly for something that might come today or in years down the road. For those of us who knew, who were open to the whisperings of the spirit, it was an agonizing time.

"We tried so hard, Rachel. We worked day and night to prepare people, to get them to listen and to believe that the world was getting ready to turn into something they could not handle alone. But most wouldn't listen. They just went right on drinking the polluted water, going to work everyday, spending their money on fashionable clothes and cars, and eating the junk food that made them obese and weak. They popped a pill when their bodies complained and pained. They would take a pill to sleep at night, they'd take a pill or drink caffeine to wake up in the morning, drink something out of a bottle when their stomach hurt from all of the abuse, constantly consumed one drug or another, then did nothing but sit in front of their TVs until it was too late to change.

"We were preaching a work ethic and a back-to-basics simplicity to a liberal, spoiled, take-what-you-can-get-for-nothing society. We were laughed at and scorned as if we were Noah building an ark, or Jeremiah prophesying that Jerusalem was to be destroyed, or yelling, "The Roman empire is about to fall," or, "beware! Hitler is trying to conquer the world...."

"...or that Jesus is about to come again," Rachel interrupted.

Michael stared in stunned silence for a moment and conceded, "Well, I see your point, but, Rachel, to me it was about getting my friends, neighbors and family to physical safety so they could still have a chance to accept truth. No amount of physical preparation will save us on that day when we are face-to-face with Jesus Christ. I know that, Rachel, but so many more could have been within walls of safety while they were learning, preparing themselves to meet Him, if they would have only listened."

Rachel saw the frustration and the pain of deep concern and caring still ablaze in Michael's eyes. A new respect blossomed within her for this good man who carried so many heavy burdens on his young shoulders. She had to make the statement that churned in her stomach, though. "Some of us never had the chance."

"I know. There were a few still out there who would listen. That's why the missionary effort continued even though it was a very dangerous world to send them into. I labored constantly for over two years, barely escaping with my life so many times, and I found two families. Peter and his companion that was killed found no one until Peter found you."

"Are there others, still?" Rachel needed to know.

"I don't think so. Ben was to be the next one from our village to go on a mission. He had already gone through all the preparations, but Adam brought news from the last conference that all missions were finished, that all the missionaries in the field were to go home to their families immediately, and there would be no more missionaries sent out."

Rachel and Michael just stared in silence, each letting the realization of it sink in. Then Rachel asked, "Was Ben relieved?"

Michael hesitated, then made the decision that he could trust Rachel to respect the intimacy of his answer. "He cried." Michael blinked a few times, looked away and breathed a deep, cleansing breath, trying to get his emotions under control. "We were all so relieved, so happy that we didn't have to send our Ben out there, but he humbled us all, when Naomi asked him why he was so sad he said, 'Because that means they're all lost, there's nobody else left to find.' We all cried then."

It was a long moment before either of them wanted to speak again, but Michael felt compelled to go on. "By the time it was clear that there were far more benefits to gathering in one place than staying in our familiar places, the roads were very hazardous to travel. There were wrecks everywhere, just left on the roads. There were hijackers on almost every highway, some posing as injured travelers and there were few gasoline stations still open. Sometimes you could go for a whole day and not find one. Even then, they would only accept cash, and sometimes they wanted clean water, food, clothes or something else they'd spot on you and demand that you give it to them in exchange for the gasoline. Like an engine part.

"No one wanted their family in two or three vehicles, either. I heard so many stories of families getting separated traveling here and never finding each other again. We were so thankful that Pops had followed his impression to buy a big old army truck with the huge canvas cover on the back. I guess they used it to haul soldiers around. It had a fuel capacity of 250 gallons which made the fuel problem manageable. Anyway, our family filled it to the top. We had to put in our food storage supplies, kitchen utensils, water, personal clothes and things, plus the easily prepared foods, sleeping gear and emergency medical supplies for the trip. We always called it our three-day emergency kit that sat by the back door at home."

When Michael smiled to himself, Rachel couldn't resist the smile that came to her own lips, and she asked, "What!"

Michael laughed then, "Well, you should have seen Naomi! Us boys stuck our pants, shirts, socks and underwear into a duffle bag, added our toothbrush, razor and aftershave, grabbed our coat, pillow and sleeping bag, and we were ready to go. It took Naomi two days to pack and she tried to bring six huge bags of clothes! She and Pops went 'round and 'round until they hit a compromise at four bags. She was thirteen then, and cried the whole trip because of the things she had to leave behind."

Rachel laughed, then asked, "Where was Christina? Didn't she complain?"

"She was too sick to care. She and Adam had just been

married a few months and she was pregnant with the twins. She threw up the whole way. Adam did all the packing. She still fusses about some of the things he left."

Rachel was beginning to see a fuller picture and she yearned to know of Michael's life before he came here. What could it have been like to grow up in a family that spoke to God, that knew how to move around safely in a world that was reeling out of control. "Where did you come from, Michael?"

"I grew up on a farm near Eugene, Idaho, in a big white farmhouse. We grew wheat and potatoes. I had planned to go to college and study agriculture, but I never got the chance."

Rachel nodded and smiled as though he had confirmed what she had suspected. Michael saw the longing and wonder in her eyes, knowing she was comparing it with the hellish childhood years she had endured, but he saw no anger there today in the depths of her eyes, he saw only the longing, a longing he wished he could fill. Oh, how he wished he could gather her into his arms and promise her he would never let her be hurt again, never leave her alone to deal in a cruel world without truth and power again. But he knew he could do no such thing, that first she must find truth and embrace it for herself, find her own power from within. Then they would be free to explore the relationship that could exist between them.

Rachel broke the silence, "How did you know where to come, and how did your group get these houses in this village?"

"Before we gathered here, we were already together all over the country in our church units at home, called wards and branches. Each geographical group of those smaller units, about eight of them, were called a stake. Our stake was in contact with the Church headquarters that had relocated from out west to here in Jackson County, Missouri. The whole process of purchasing and selling began years before. We gave up a 120 acre farm for two small community houses, because Pops knew what was really important and how it would be. We were all taught, slowly, to live the Law of Consecration so we would be able to live together here in harmony when the time came. If we chose to, of course."

Rachel thought that over for a few minutes, then offered, "I bet the greedy ones loved that, huh?"

Michael raised a brow at her insight, and marveled again at how far she had come in the few months he had known her. "So you know what the Law of Consecration is?"

"I didn't know what it was called, but now that I'm living it here, it's easy for me to say it's good, because I have gained everything and given nothin'." Rachel lowered her head as if she were ashamed.

Michael reached over and took her hand in his and lifted her chin with his other hand. He searched her eyes until she gave him her full attention. "Rachel, you're wrong about that. You've given the most important thing you have to give, the one thing God desires the most from you. The thing that makes a thousand acres pale in comparison. You've given your heart."

Chapter 10

Rachel looked around the table at everyone happily eating the meal she'd prepared and smiled with satisfaction. She had been a nervous wreck ever since she invited Michael and his family to dinner. She'd done it in a weak moment after their satisfying talk a few days ago. Michael had made her feel so good about herself that she had imagined she could do anything. Like cook dinner for eighteen people. But here they sat, all gathered around Grampy and Grandmother William's beautiful old oak table, everyone eating with enthusiasm and talking to each other as though they were lifelong friends. Rachel's eyes drifted to Michael's the same instant he looked over at her. He beamed a full, white grin of approval that was so endearing it made her blush, but she returned it heartily.

Ben made a big show of patting his stomach and giving a big, satisfied stretch while grinning at Sarah. Rachel noticed that Sarah had some tint in her cheeks as well, and was finally able to smile about her little sister's impending romance with the handsome young villager. Suddenly Ben's attentions switched to Rachel. "Rach, you done good! I don't think anybody in this village knows how to fry chicken like that, and I can't believe you even made turnips taste good!"

Anxious to divert all of the attention that was suddenly coming her way, Rachel said, "Thank you, Ben, but a lot of the credit goes to Sarah and Daniel. Daniel has grease burns all over his arms 'cause we had the stove too hot. Everybody else helped, too. Ginny set the table, and Troy and William peeled all the vegetables."

When Rachel looked at Joe hesitantly, not knowing

what to say for him since he'd refused to help, he mocked, "And I ain't takin' no credit 'cause I ain't never doin' nothin' to help you when you're entertainin' these...."

When Joe saw Troy's eyes go hard with warning, he amended what he was about to say even though it turned his stomach to do it, "...when you're throwin' such a big party. I guess I thought I'd mess it up, is all." He looked down at his plate and started eating again.

After a minute of awkward silence, Ben saved the day, "Well, let me tell you! I can't help but remember when we first got here. I was only eleven years old, and few things are as important to an eleven year old as his stomach, and mine was sorely neglected in my mind."

Everyone laughed even before he finished his story because they all knew Ben was still ruled by his stomach. He continued, "It took us three days of hard driving to get here from Idaho. Pops didn't think it was safe to build a fire and draw attention to ourselves and all the provisions on the truck, so we ate cold food the whole time! Those dry army meals were kinda fun the first day, but by the second day I felt like I was stuffing a pound of crackers in my mouth then trying to wash it down with a teaspoon of water."

Pops hooted and chided, "Well I guess you did, son. It was all the rest of us could do to stuff one-half of one of those meals into our mouths, and you managed to stuff the whole thing in yours in half the time!" Pops slapped his knee and laughed again at the memory. "Then you wanted Naomi's share of the water since she was a girl and couldn't possibly need all of the nourishment that a big man like you needed."

Everyone enjoyed teasing Ben since he seemed to be enjoying it as much as they were, so it continued. Michael added, "It wasn't just Naomi's water he was after. I ended up with four of his Snickers bars for one cup of my Kool-Aid water! He still throws that up to me when he gets mad at me. Says I took advantage of him."

Mama couldn't help adding to the laughter, "Well, the worst part is what happens to a person when they eat too much dehydrated food without drinking enough water. Ben had enough water rationed to him, mind you, and all the rest of us did fine. He just didn't quit eating when his stomach was full, so the second day I had to dip into my emergency medical supplies and help him out with a laxative."

Christina managed to get her dig in between laughs, "That's why we didn't get here until late the third day, because we had to stop a million times for Ben to run to the bushes. Mama told him to only take one square of the choco-late-flavored laxative, and that's all he ate while she was watching, but Ben snuck and took another one when she walked off, because he thought it tasted good."

After that round of laughter eased, Christina continued, "The worse part was every time he started holding his stomach and banging on the truck for Pops to stop, my own nausea would flare up just thinking about what he was going to do. I was pregnant with the twins, you see, so every time Ben ran to the bushes, I was right behind him throwing up."

Adam looked at Christina with affection and teased, "You cannot imagine how upset I was that my beautiful new bride had turned a shade of pale green and had decided she didn't like me or anyone else. Back then I couldn't figure it all out, but now we're pros at this morning sickness thing, this time it is a lot easier...."

Adam realized too late he had said too much when Mama and Naomi squeaked, "Another baby!"

Christina smiled at their enthusiasm, and answered with a nod while she poked Adam in the ribs at the same time for telling their little secret. She added, "I didn't know for sure until last week after I visited the doctor. I couldn't believe I was pregnant because I wasn't sick!"

Naomi pouted, "I should have been the first to know." But she laughed when Peter gave her a pouty lip and mouthed, "Poor baby."

Christina poked Adam again, "Well, you would have been the first to know if Adam hadn't blurted it out just now. I was going to tell you tonight and then we could have announced it at Monday's family meeting."

"Are we going to get more babies?" asked Jeremy.

No one had really considered the other children's feel-ings until Jeremy spoke. Adam decided he should answer since this had been his blunder, "Yep, sport. We're going to have us another little friend to play with."

Jeremy shouted, "Yeepee!"

Everyone laughed, but Christina was the first to notice Amy and Paul just sitting there looking at each other sadly. "What's wrong, guys?" When they didn't say anything, Christina added, "You can tell Mommy."

Amy began hesitantly, "Will you be like you were with Jeremy and Jeremiah?"

Christina became a little embarrassed at the question, knowing they were talking about her throwing up and being in bed so much, and probably how grouchy she became for a while. But she sighed and figured she should just as well say it to everyone. "Well, honey, I think it will be much better this time. You see, Mommy isn't nearly as sick as the other times...and I'm older and smarter now, too, so when I get tired I'll just call for a fun storytime or a visit to Grandmama's house instead of getting grouchy. Okay?"

Paul smiled tentatively, but asked, "What if the new baby wants you to lug it around like Jeremiah does? Your back ain't strong enough for that, Mommy."

Christina smiled at her little man's concern, ignoring his use of the word ain't for once, and answered, "Well, we never know exactly which special spirit Heavenly Father will send us, or what his needs will be, but whoever it is we'll be honored to have him or her and help him to grow during his earth life. Besides, look how big you and Amy are now! You'll be able to help a lot, so we'll just teach the baby from the beginning that it has to share its hugs and snuggles with you two just as much as it shares them with me, okay?"

Amy and Paul looked at each other just like they always did when either one of them was trying to make a decision. It was as if they needed each other to be complete. Slowly, the grins began to form on their faces, then they both answered gleefully at the same time, "Okay, you can have another baby!"

Rachel watched with open admiration how the little family and the members in it dealt openly and honestly with each other, and especially how they managed to do it in kindness. She bounced Jeremiah on her knee, where he had been for the last ten minutes. He had just toddled over and tugged at her leg, something he had never done before. Somehow she knew she'd be seeing a lot of the little guy in the next few weeks while Christina wasn't feeling her best. It brought her a deep sense of belonging and usefulness that prompted her to snuggle him a little tighter and give him a big kiss on his chubby little cheek.

Ben suddenly stated, "Hey, I was right in the middle of a story before King Adam announced an increase in his kingdom. May I continue now?"

Adam made a gallant gesture for Ben to continue, spreading his arm out to the side, nearly taking Ben's nose with it. After they shared a moment of pure brother-to-brother arm pounding, Ben picked up the story. "Anyway, I had never been so happy to arrive at a place in my life when we got here. That truck had beat all of us into a million pieces, not to mention the tension that was always there while we traveled through what looked like a war zone. The thought was always there that somebody was going to jump us."

Naomi cut in, "You're not fooling anybody, Ben. The only thing that scared you was losing your food stash! Do you guys remember the time we filled up with gasoline and the station owner wanted some junk food as well as the cash? We were all so grateful to even find a station open that we gladly dipped into our bags and pulled out a candy bar, trail mix and fruit, stuff like that. Well, Pops had to take Ben's out of his bag for him. He just couldn't bring himself to give it up!"

Ben retorted, "Well, what did you expect? We didn't get a lot of that junk food on the farm, it was my private treasure. Besides, I couldn't fill up on the dehydrated food anymore, so my private stash was my only hope! And Pops wanted me to give it away to a greasy gas guy."

All three of the Rock men, Pops, Adam and Michael, slapped their legs and hooted at the same time. The women giggled with pleasure at how serious Ben had become over an incident almost seven years before. The children even laughed at the image of their big, strong uncle fretting over giving away his candy bar to a greasy stranger.

Ben decided he couldn't let them get the best of him, so he grinned and continued, "I thought it would be just like it used to be when we got here. But, man oh man, was I surprised! There wasn't anything here but a bunch of empty houses and the Williams'. We couldn't bring any livestock or fresh meat, and I don't mind telling you I had a bad hankering for a big juicy steak like we had on the farm all the time. Or a baked chicken, or an orange pheasant, or a lamb chop, but what I got was cracked wheat and some bread, and a whole lot of work for the next year."

Daniel joined in for the first time, though he had been laughing during Ben's whole story, "How did you get all the things for buildin' all the greenhouses? And how'd you end up with the barn animals and enough food and water for everythin'?"

Ben answered, "The members of the Church had been taught to store a year's supply of their favorite foods that would keep well, and to grow gardens and sew their own clothes, stuff like that, for as long as I can remember, but I don't mind telling you that I thought it was a waste of time when Pops and Mama insisted we help them build and run a little greenhouse. After all, we plowed a hundred acres and always had a ton of food, so I didn't see the point. But it became more and more clear as each family brought their little greenhouse with them and added it to ours. Not every family could, of course, but I realize now that the experience we gained was essential. It eased the fear a lot just to understand what we needed to do.

"I guess our parents didn't want to scare us with the

harsh truth of what it was going to be like. I was just young and wanted a steak."

Everyone fell silent for a moment, each allowing themselves to mourn a little for the loss of those naive days of plenty.

"Anyway," Ben continued, "Pops and the Church leaders had it all worked out that there would be some livestock here from some of the other established villages or members to get our village barn going, so my first assignment was to take over for the Williams and clean the barn. I want you to know that my first desire was to murder me a pig and have some pork chops. But Pops patiently explained that we needed to get the stock built up first, so we could eventually feed and care for all of the families that would be moving here from our church ward back home. He also explained that there were many valuable things that came from the animals besides their meat, like their milk, skins and furs. But like I said, the only big picture I had was of a big plate of food."

Everyone was a little surprised when Troy joined in the story and asked, "You mean there's other villages like this one?"

Pops decided to answer, "There's hundreds of them all over the world, Troy, though most of them in this country are centered around this county, here in Missouri. There are a lot of benefits in being this close to the Church headquarters and the information that comes from the conferences, not to mention the safety in the numbers here. There are some scattered in other states, but most of the wards and branches of the Church chose to come here. Plus there are many other groups, mostly religious based ones, that have organized, too."

William shocked everybody by summing it up nicely, "In other words, we are all a part of Jesus's Church and he's wantin' to look out for us if we'll just let him by listenin' to what he tells his leaders." After a moment of silence, he added, "And I don't mind tellin' you I'm mighty glad to be here!"

Ginny looked at her man with so much pride that it began to drip from her eyes.

Sarah hadn't said a word up to this point, but she got up and walked over to William and kissed him on the cheek and said softly, "Me, too."

Sarah started clearing the dishes from the table and asked, "Ya'll ready for desert? It's homemade brownies with hot fudge sauce and whipped cream. We've saved our cocoa allowance for two weeks, especially for tonight!"

Everyone fretted over their full stomachs and moaned with pleasure as their mouths watered at the prospect of such a treat. But the evening suddenly took a turn for the worst when Joe finally took his turn at speaking.

Joe demanded in a loud, angry voice, "Rachel, you really want'a know why I can't stand you scrawny little witch and...and why Daniel can't stand his sweet littl' sister?"

Everyone else was too stunned to say or do anything, but Troy was on his feet in an instant, and Daniel was shouting at Joe, "You leave me out of this! What I told you ain't suppose' to be repeated. If you do, I'm gonna smash your mean littl' head!" When Daniel got up out of his seat, too, Rachel simply motioned with her hand for both of them to sit back down. It had been a while since Rachel had used the signals, and it had been a while since the men had heeded them, but both acted automatically. Too many times their lives had depended on strict adherence, and none of them felt safe enough in the village to completely abandon their old ways yet.

Michael watched as the commanded silence fell upon the room. Not even Joe spoke a word while Rachel studied him. Michael marveled, even in the midst of the tangible tension, how natural a leader Rachel was. In that instant he found himself quite comfortable with allowing Rachel to handle it her way. He realized he trusted her judgement completely. He almost smiled when it dawned on him that most of her bluster was reserved for him, because he had never seen her rattled when it really counted.

She spoke quietly, but firmly. She was surprised and proud of herself at the same time for the willingness and security she felt in allowing Joe to speak his mind. "Go ahead, Joe. I do want to know."

After a moment of shock at being allowed to continue with his mutiny, Joe spat, "Well, I'll jus' tell ya. You know when your Paw used to disappear, sometimes for days, after you'd make him so mad with your prissy littl' protective ways over that no-account Sarah?"

Everyone sat silently, waiting for Rachel to react.

She was glad Joe was finally talking, she was strangely calm about it, and she didn't want him to quit, but she just couldn't see airing her problems in front of Michael's family, especially if it involved her Paw.

Pops seemed to sense her dilemma, so he offered, "We could leave, Rachel, it's late anyway."

Joe responded loudly, "No! If you leave, I'll not finish."

Rachel realized immediately that Joe was afraid of Troy and Daniel who were still eyeing him viciously. She silenced their threats with one swift, hard look at each of them. They immediately looked away, but Daniel got up and headed out the door. Rachel allowed him to do that without protest, then spoke, "I don't care if they all stay, Joe, but I won't force them to stay and hear this if they want to leave."

Joe nodded his acceptance, feeling better that Rachel had assured his safety with the two men who would love to hurt him. He had been hurt enough in his life, he didn't think he could stand any more. When nobody got up to leave, he continued, "Do you know where you run him off to? Do you care?"

Joe was more emotional than Rachel had ever seen him, he was visibly shaking, and she sensed he was close to tears. She consciously spoke quietly, calmly, "Where, Joe. Where'd he go?"

"He'd come back to his Maw's 'bout ten miles south in the woods, and...and he was real mean to her...and he'd jus' keep drinkin' and cussin' 'bout that devil daughter of his that kept tryin' to kill him. He'd jus' get meaner and meaner no matter what...what she did for him. He hurt her real bad."

Rachel was so confused. Maw Bentley? She'd been dead for years. Her whole family had gone to the funeral right after they'd moved to Minnesota. She still remembered holding onto Sarah, and how glad she was that her Mama had held onto Daniel that day and kept him away from their Paw. He had been drunk even for his own mother's funeral.

Rachel asked, "Joe, how did he hurt her? What did he do?"

"He...he made her cook for him...and...and give him baths...."

Rachel asked, "What else, Joe?"

"And she had to take her...her clothes off, too, and he...he beat her when she said No!"

Rachel went pale when the little whisper came to her. She lowered her eyes and asked the question, "Where was you, Joe, when Paw was bein' mean to Maw Bentley?"

Joe looked confused for a moment, then looked straight into Rachel's eyes as she met his, and he found the strength there to say the words, "I was there."

Rachel continued, "But Maw Bentley was already dead, right, Joe?"

Finally all the hate and hurt spilled out of his eyes onto his cheeks, and Joe answered, "Yeah, she was dead."

Michael looked around to see if the others were as confused as he was, and it was obvious they were. But he became filled with concern when he saw how pale Sarah had become. She looked so frightened and vulnerable. He looked over at Ben and saw the deep concern on his face as he eyed Sarah.

Suddenly, Sarah stood up and screamed at Joe, "It was you! You was the one he hurt." She lowered her voice as she sat back down and said in nearly a whisper, "Just like it was me he hurt."

Ben moved swiftly to Sarah's chair and she leaned into his shoulder and wept bitterly.

"And me," Daniel added from the doorway. "The bastard hurt all of us."

Rachel lowered her head and sobbed into her hands. Michael was kneeling by her side before the first teardrop hit the table, soothing her, telling her it wasn't her fault, but she screamed at him, "It *was* my fault, I didn't stop him!"

Daniel spoke again, determined to finally get it all out, "Everytime you took Sarah and ran with her, he'd come after me. I hated Sarah all these years 'cause you cared more about her. You took her and left me."

Rachel stared at her brother through tear-stained eyes, "Dear God! Daniel, I...I didn't know...you were a boy...and I didn't think he would...."

Daniel said sadly, all of the hatred he'd felt for years finally leaving him, "It didn't matter to him what I was."

Joe stammered, "Daniel, you jus' said he beat you 'cause...'cause Sarah was gone...."

"He did the same things to me that he did to you," Daniel supplied. "The only difference is you was his brother."

Rachel stared from one to the other, then looked at Joe, "You're Billy Joe, Paw's little brother who lived in Wisconsin?"

Joe just nodded. "I came back after Maw Bentley died. She left me the home place. I thought ya'll knew I was there."

The twins whimpered and everyone turned at the same time to look at them. Christina was by their side immediately, telling them she was sorry for not paying more attention to their feelings, and it was time to go home. They got up willingly and Adam joined them and picked Amy up into his arms where she immediately fell into a deeper sob at his neck, wrapping both arms around him tightly. Christina tucked Paul into her side and he, too, wrapped his arms tightly around his protector's waist. He looked up into her face and asked, "You won't let that happen to me, will you Mommy?"

Before Christina could answer, Joe answered in the first kind voice anyone had ever heard him use, "He will never hurt you, buddy, 'cause I...." He looked uncertain for a minute, then decided to just say it. "I made sure he'd never hurt anyone again. He's dead and burned, and payin' for what he done. Okay?"

Paul nodded and reached out and took Joe's hand as he walked by. He looked up into Joe's face and said, "I'm sorry that happened to you, but you will be okay now that you are here with us. Will you come tomorrow and show me how to make a booby trap for a rabbit that's eating my Mommy's flowers?"

Joe actually grinned when he answered, "Sure, buddy." But he quickly became serious again after Adam and Christina left. He looked at Rachel and finished, "I thought your mama would just get up and walk out after I set the fire...but she just sat there with his dead body. I never meant to hurt her, Rachel, and I thought she'd bring you kids and come and stay with me...and I'd take care of you. But I guess you didn't even know I was there...and when you took off, I thought you knew what I done, so I just followed you. I don't know why. You was all I had left."

There was silence after that until Pops got up from his position at the table and walked straight over to Rachel, stood her up, and proceeded to embrace her in a bear hug that only a father could give. He promised, "From this day forward, I will be the father you never had, and Mama the mother you never had, and I swear to you it will be good. Is that okay with you?"

Rachel nodded her head where it leaned against Pop's massive chest. He pulled her away and lifted her chin to look into his eyes, "I love you, Rachel. You're a good person and I'm honored to have you in my family. There's a lot of healing yet to come, but it was a good beginning tonight. We'll talk about appointments that will help tomorrow, Rachel, and we'll be here for you—for all of you."

Mama and Naomi hugged each one of them, and soon the room was empty of Rocks except for Michael and Ben. When Rachel and Sarah began clearing the table, and

Michael and Ben, along with William and Ginny, had just started pitching in, Joe took the dish from Rachel's hand and offered, "I'd like to do the cleanin' up since I didn't do nothin' to help earlier."

When Rachel surveyed the massive mess and began to look uncertain, Daniel added, "I'll help, too. You bunch of lovebirds go take a walk." His handsome young grin had them all smiling sheepishly. His eyes lingered on Ginny just a moment too long.

Troy threw in, "Well, I'll help too, since the lovebirds surely ain't got no use fer me!" He laughed one of his rare, rotten-toothed laughs and slapped his knee in mimic of Pops, which had everyone loosened up and laughing within seconds.

Ben motioned toward the door and he and Sarah disappeared without a word, Sarah still rubbing the tears from her eyes.

William took Ginny by the hand and said, "It's been a long time since me and Ginny's took a walk. I think we jus' might take one." With that, he grinned broadly and ushered Ginny out the door. Only Michael caught the longing look Ginny gave Daniel as she followed William out the door.

Rachel looked at Joe and their eyes met in a silent truce. She really wanted to go over and give him a big hug, tell him she forgave him, and tell him how sorry she was for everything bad that had ever happened to him. But she knew that would have to come later, neither was ready for that yet, so she simply gave a small, sincere smile that Joe returned in good measure.

The awkward silence that followed prompted Michael to venture, "Well, little lovebird, could I interest you in a trip to the barn to check on Dizzy Lizzy and her two ping-pong balls? One of the fillies has a cut on her leg that needs some ointment."

"Let me warn you, Michael, I don't feel like anybody's lovebird right now, but you did just mention the one place that I wouldn't mind goin' to right now."

As they walked down the steps of the beautiful old front porch, they saw Ben and Sarah at the park across the street, sitting in the swing. Ben had his arm draped casually around Sarah's shoulder and was listening intently to whatever she was saying. For some reason, it didn't bother Rachel that Sarah was receiving her solace from Ben tonight. It suddenly seemed like a very good thing. She looked up at Michael as he draped his arm around her shoulders and asked, "Do you think it's a good thing?"

Michael didn't need to ask what she meant, as was usually the case with them. He looked back at Sarah and Ben and stated, "It's a very good thing."

Sarah finally noticed Rachel and Michael as they headed for the barn. A little smile formed through her tears, and Ben asked, "What?"

Ben followed her gaze and gave a little smile himself.

"Do you think it is a good thing?" Sarah asked.

Ben's smile widened to a full white grin when he answered, "I can safely say that Rachel is the best thing that could have ever happened to my far-too-serious brother. She challenged his perfect little order with her sexy little chaos."

Sarah looked alarmed, "You don't think they have...."

Ben cut in, "Of course not! But she made him really want to, and that's okay as long as you control it. It's no different than how I feel about you."

Ben's tone had suddenly gotten very serious and Sarah looked at him in surprise. Ben had never once come right out and told her that he cared for her.

Sarah's look of surprise made Ben feel ashamed for being such a coward about his feelings for her. It gave him the courage he needed to say what was on his mind finally, "I think I'm in love with you, Sarah. It's just we're so young...and I've been afraid of how strongly I feel for you, and afraid I'd have to leave you soon to go on a mission, and make no mistake, Sarah, I would have gone if I'd been called to go."

Ben squeezed Sarah's hands so hard that it hurt as he

continued, "I was...am afraid that you don't feel as strongly as I do...and I don't know if I could deal with it if you didn't feel the same, about a lot of things, I guess, and I know that it probably isn't fair to expect that you feel the same as I do...about life...and things."

"Why ain't it fair?" Sarah retorted. "I wouldn't want you if you didn't see life out of the same book as I did."

Ben looked a little confused, so Sarah clarified, "The scriptures. You know, our script for life. Peter explained it to us. If you run around in life without your script, you won't know what your part in life is. I've been a part of that world that runs around without a script my whole life. I hated it. It's sad and awful, and it really scares me to think that Peter almost didn't find us. Anyway, I wouldn't want a man that didn't know what his part in life really is. You know, Ben. And Michael knows. If you hadn't been willin' to go on your mission, you wouldn't be the man I thought you was...were."

Sarah looked away a little embarrassed to have been so forward with Ben and to have corrected her improper language in front of him. No one knew she and Rachel sat together at night and challenged each other in word games that helped them to correct the poor language their parents had left them with, but she forced herself to add anyway, "I know I'm in love with you, Ben. And...and I'm glad you didn't have to go away."

Since Ben had no words to describe how wonderful and relieved he felt at what Sarah had just said, he did what he had desired to do for so long. He lifted Sarah's chin and looked into her soul with his soft, chocolate-brown eyes that looked just like Mama's. He lowered his lips to Sarah's and kissed her gently, reverently.

Sarah ran her fingers through his beautiful, tawny hair, but felt Ben's caution, his worry, and knew they had to talk about it, get it out in the open, right now, tonight. Since she couldn't imagine where to begin or how to talk about something like that, she just took a deep, shaky breath and blurted it out, "I knew it before tonight, Ben. I knew what my Paw used to do to me. I have nightmares about it...but I just wouldn't ever deal with it...it hurt too bad...and I didn't have any real reason to deal with it until I met you. Then you became the biggest reason to pretend it never happened...because I thought you wouldn't want me if you knew."

Ben took her into his arms and held her tightly, soothing, "You know I still want you, Sarah. I'll always want you." He fell silent and wondered how he could ask her the question that burned in his stomach.

"But?" Sarah knew Ben needed to say more.

"But will you still want me...a man...after what he did to you?" Ben felt the chill quake through his body as he fought with the anger he felt for the dead man who had hurt his Sarah so completely, so thoroughly, who had taken from her as a child what should have been hers to give to him as a woman.

"When I'm with you, I don't remember it, Ben. When I'm around other men, out there, it's all around me...I'm always frightened. But I feel safe here, safe with you. I've never been afraid of you."

Somehow she still had not said what he needed to hear. He knew he was a man of passion. Unlike Michael, he had fought for control for years. He was proud to say he had won the battle so far, knowing and honoring the deep respect his parents had taught him for women and the sacredness of marriage, and, as well, the relationship between men and women, and the precious responsibility and opportunity that children brought to such a union. "But will you want me, Sarah, really want me, like Christina wants Adam, like a man and woman want each other? Will it still be a wonderful thing...after...."

Sarah knew she was on dangerous ground. The prompting she was receiving could be temptation, could be evil, and if she followed it she might ruin everything between her and Ben. She was so inexperienced in distinguishing good from evil. She closed her eyes and prayed for help, *Please help me to know what to do, what to say, and to be a good woman, for myself, and for Ben.*

Ben tensed as he felt Sarah withdraw. He had pushed her too far, too quick. Hang his needs and his passion, he should be thinking about her, giving her all the time she needed to become whole again. But, Oh God, he knew how important this was, to his eternal happiness, and hers. He had a right to know where he stood, what to expect. Or not to expect.

Sarah opened her eyes and saw the pain, the uncertainty in Ben's handsome face. She never wanted to see that look again. Never wanted to be the source of his uncertainty again, ever. She leaned forward and pulled his lips to hers. It was all so very tentative at first, then Ben teased at the corner of her lips and she opened them willingly and gave him something that she had never offered before, knew she would never offer to any other man. The sensations, the overpowering urge to move closer was wonderful, consuming.

Ben shifted and pulled her more fully into his arms and trailed kisses across her forehead, down her nose, then once again claimed what he had desired for so long in her lips. His hand moved slowly, sensuously up and down the length of her arm and she gave fully, completely.

Sarah had never felt so right, so cleansed. She could finally allow herself to feel, to really feel without shame, pain and regret. She had known it would be this way with Ben, knew it because she had spent long hours on her knees praying for it, praying that God would not allow her past to control her future, and He had granted it to her.

She knew they should pull away, should not allow their passion to become wrong, to turn a wonderful blessing into a thing of sin, but Sarah knew it had to be Ben that pulled them back. She prayed again, silently in her heart, fervently, *Please help Ben to do what's right.*

Ben reluctantly stilled the kiss that had moved his soul, that had let him know he held the right woman, a good woman who matched his passion, his enthusiasm and determination, in every way. An equal mate to share all time with.

He looked into her eyes and reveled at the passion and love held in them for him. He moved, swiftly, efficiently onto one knee while he held her hand, and gazed into her love-filled eyes with a happiness in his own that only a man in love can have. "Sarah, honey, I know we're not ready quite yet, but when we are, when you are ready, will you be my wife, be my partner for all eternity?"

Through tears of joy and soft, nubbing sobs, Sarah nodded her consent.

Chapter 11

After caring for Princess Mocha's baby, Michael and Rachel sat in the clean hay in the corner and enjoyed the simplicity of the moment. Rachel began thinking out loud, "I can see the benefits to being an animal. One that's cared for, anyway. No decisions, no worry, no thinking." Rachel sighed and continued to give voice to her thoughts, perfectly at ease doing it right in front of Michael. "No choices, no growing."

Michael sensed the change in direction and added his concurrence, "No ability to act, always being acted upon."

Rachel smiled and added, "No ability to argue when you disagree."

Michael smiled, "No ability to choose who you sit in the hay with."

Rachel laughed, "Yeah, well, sometimes that might be a good thing!"

Michael feigned offense, "Are you suggesting I'm not a perfect person for you to sit in the hay with?"

"Pops would be safer. Or Troy. Or Grampy. Ben. Anybody besides you!" Rachel laughed and sneered at the same time, then scooted away to make her point.

"So you are crazy about me?" Michael slapped his knee and said, "I knew it!"

Rachel became a little more serious than she had intended, "And are you crazy about me?"

Michael looked away and fell silent. Just when Rachel was feeling completely embarrassed and considering making her escape in anger, Michael turned and looked her square in the face, and didn't blink when he stated, "I'm crazy about you and everything I see you becoming. I just hope I can keep up. You grow a lot faster than I do. I'm kinda stuck in my ways."

Rachel stared at this man, a man she admired above all others, one she had come to respect completely because he was good and honest, open and up front in everything he said and did. She knew she could believe what he had just confessed, take it as fact that it was exactly how he felt. There was just one thing she needed to qualify before she allowed the tiny hope burning within her to blossom. "What exactly does it mean to be crazy about someone, Michael?"

Michael looked at her and realized that she was finally opening up to him, finally willing to allow the relationship she had fought for so long to begin. He knew a moment of uncertainty, a moment of complete vulnerability, but what was new about that with Rachel? In that few seconds of time he decided to throw caution to the wind and spell it out, to finally say what was in his heart and accept whatever happened next.

After getting up and positioning himself on both knees in front of her, Michael took Rachel's hands in his and declared, "It means I am deeply and completely in love with you, Rachel. It means I would like to ask you to be my equal partner, for all time and throughout all eternity. I want you...I need you to be my wife. It means I would like to have lots of babies with you, and be by your side as we raise them to be good and happy."

The tears flowed freely from Rachel's eyes without embarrassment for the first time in her life. She reached out and touched Michael's cheek and looked into his eyes and asked, "You really want to have a bunch of ping-pong balls with me?"

Michael smiled through the burning that was just barely contained behind his eye lids, "More than anything in this world."

Rachel looked into his eyes and smiled, but the smile faded and pure sadness settled into the depths of them. She looked away for a minute, then back again with a fear in them that was tangible, one more potent than Michael had ever seen in them, more powerful than that of facing a wolverine. She tried desperately to control the sobs that mingled with her words, "I'm so scared I'll let you down, Michael. I've watched you, I know what you do. I'm afraid I won't be strong enough to do all of those things. I get so angry, and you're the most even person I've ever met. Well, except with me sometimes, but that's because you are romantically involved with me and that makes people act a little crazy sometimes."

Michael smiled over that little bit of wisdom, but he squeezed her hands, encouraging her to continue. "I've changed my mind about all the little circles you run in everyday, you know, the ones I thought were so silly...and that I thought were weaknesses. Praying, reading the scriptures, exercising, eating just right, going to all of your meetings, doing everything on your list everyday. You do them because they keep you safe, keep you on the right track. You keep yourself so busy doing good and righteous things, helping everybody all the time, that bad things just can't edge their way in. Oh, I know you get tempted, I'm not meaning to discredit the strength it takes for you to do it every day."

Rachel looked frustrated, like she wasn't getting out what she really wanted to say. "Michael, I lived the first sixteen years of my life with a mean drunk, just trying to survive. I've lived the other six years of my life on the road sleeping under trees, just trying to survive but I did whatever I wanted to do, I went wherever I wanted to go. There were only two things that ever really meant anything to me, Sarah and Daniel, and finding pure water and I don't even know why I wanted to find that water so badly.

"Every time somebody would tell us they'd heard of good water here or there, I'd drag us off after it, not even knowin' what difference it'd make after I found it. We've learned to filter the nasty stuff and survive without the pure water, so it doesn't even make any sense what I was doing."

Michael interrupted, "Well, it makes perfect sense to me."

171

Rachel stilled, "It does?"

"Rachel, listen. I know when you compare what you have done with what you still have to do yet, it scares you, you feel inadequate. Please trust me when I tell you we all feel that way sometimes, no one is completely secure with their righteousness, we have to work hard at it everyday. But look at what you have become on your own, just you, without loving parents and without the truth of why you are here on earth, things I have had my whole life.

"You loved your little sister and brother, even though you'd been shown no love. You took them away and took care of them even though no one ever took care of you, and of course you searched for pure water, it was the only thing that represented goodness and pureness to you. But the real point is that you wanted that goodness and pureness, Rachel, and God knew you wanted it, so He led you here. And the real miracle is that you collected the few that were left out there that were seeking the truth too, and brought them along with you."

Michael sighed and looked away in shame, "The thing I am so sorry for is that a wolverine trying to take a precious little boy's life and the angry world trying to take away the best missionary I've ever met, had to be thrown at us before we could even see you for what you were."

Rachel, sobbing even more now, so full of love and appreciation for this man who saw so much, who miraculously loved her, found the courage to ask one last time, "You are sure you want me, Michael? And you are sure I can be this equal partner, this wife that you have waited so long for, the one you have cherished in your heart since you were a child?"

When Michael started to answer, Rachel interrupted, "Be certain before you answer, Michael, because I never give up something once it's mine."

Michael wiped her tears away with a gentle finger and smiled, "I have always been yours, it has just taken us awhile to admit it and deal with it. Now, I am going to be the one to ask this question, not you. Do you understand?"

Rachel nodded, relieved to finally have someone in her life with strength and honor that she could turn to, someone who would demand his place, his role, but with kindness and integrity.

"Will you marry me, Rachel? Will you walk with me, by my side, forever?"

There would be no more doubting, no more backing away from what lay ahead. She would meet it head-on, as she had everything else that had really challenged her in her life. Only this time, she realized, she wasn't afraid anymore. She had Michael. And the truth. There was nothing more she needed, other than what had to come from within her. And Michael had just helped her to realize she was good inside. She had never been more certain of anything in her life when she answered, "With honor, Michael. I will walk beside you with honor."

Nothing could have stopped the flow that seeped from Michael's eyes as he heard the words he had waited so long to hear. He would have a family soon, with Rachel. It was almost too much to believe. He knew Rachel had set her will in motion, he had seen the determination take over, as he had known it would. He trusted her and it humbled him to know how much she trusted him.

It would be a good marriage, full of challenge and passion and he looked forward to every moment of it. But what he said addressed the issue that paled all other concerns, "I promise you we will be ready, Rachel. We will be ready to meet our Savior together when he comes again. I know we're not ready to be married right now, but we will talk to the Bishop tomorrow and start our preparations to go to the temple as soon as we can, okay?"

Rachel nodded. Then Michael drew them into a tight, hope-filled embrace, so different from the ones they'd shared before, yet so perfect.

* * * *

William and Ginny inspected the ripe, juicy tomatoes and marveled that they existed this late in the year, marveled that they existed at all. William pointed out, "See, these are startin' to fade out, they've produced a lot a'ready, so Michael had us plant new seeds a few weeks back." He pointed to another section which housed the young plants. "Those will be ready to produce by the time these give out completely. Michael's real smart. I like learnin' from him."

Ginny added, "Everybody here smart. Good place to be. Ginny like it." She smiled up at William and said, "Ginny like you, too."

William let go of Ginny's hand and wandered off, aimlessly, knowing he had to put some distance between them. When he finally looked back and saw the hurt in her eyes, he came to her quickly and picked her up and sat her on one of the tables. He raised her chin gently and said, "I'm sorry, Ginny. I didn't mean to be hateful or anythin'. I'm just so confused."

Ginny nodded and said, "Me, too."

William hesitated, a little relieved to know she was feeling it too. "I've never asked, Ginny, but I would like to know, how old are you?"

"Sixteen summers," Ginny bragged.

William looked away in shame, Ginny confirming what he had started to suspect.

Ginny broke the silence, "How many summers for you?"

"Twenty-nine."

"My mother was at start of thirty-two summer." Ginny looked away, suddenly feeling awkward with William, and sad to think of her mother that she still missed so much.

William finally found the courage to say, "It was wrong what we did, Ginny. Those nights in the woods. I'm sorry."

"Ginny know. Ginny sorry, too."

"Please forgive me, Ginny. I didn't know what I know

now, or I never would have...." William looked at his feet, unable to look Ginny in the eye.

Ginny's eyes were wet when she forced William to look at her again, but she said with a steady voice, "You best friend Ginny ever had. You there when heart nearly break, you good man. We make mistake, we forget, do better now."

William stuttered, "What...what about us...will we...."

"We be best friends, that all, okay?" Ginny asked.

William smiled, relieved. Then he blurted before he thought, "Now you and Daniel can like each other."

Ginny's eyes grew wide, then she laughed, "How you know what Ginny not say to anyone."

William laughed, "You can't keep much from me. I'm too big, I'm everywhere!"

"Well, Ginny pretty small, but she see things everywhere, too. You like lady whose husband die," Ginny waggled a good natured finger at him.

"Is...is that okay, Ginny? You're not mad?" William asked.

"Ginny happy for you, you good friend. Lady really like you. Lady's little boy really like you. You make good father."

William grabbed her up and twirled her around until they were both dizzy.

They were giggling loudly when Rachel and Michael opened the door and walked into the balmy warmth of the greenhouse. "Well, it looks like you two are feeling happy," Michael teased.

William set Ginny down and she blurted, "We work it all out. We make mistakes, but we forget and do better. William like widow lady and I like Daniel. We best friends still."

William smiled happily until he saw the worry on Rachel's face. "Is that okay, Rachel," he asked uncertainly.

Rachel's features softened when she looked at both of them and said, "Thank you for asking, William, but I shouldn't be tellin' you what to do anymore. You're an adult, you have to decide."

William's eyes filled with the pride he was beginning to develop in himself, and with the love he felt for Rachel. He stated, "You've been a good leader, Rachel. You brought us here. You saved all of us. I will always respect what you say, even though I might not always have the smarts to follow it." He reached out his massive, beefy arms and gave her a huge bear hug.

When the friendly gestures ceased, Rachel looked to Michael for some help, as she began, "Michael could get you both set up with the Bishop so you can get everything worked out...so you can get it all out in the open and make it right."

Michael offered, "I'll be glad to do that for both of you."

William looked at Ginny warily, then asked Rachel reluctantly, "It's what we need to do, then?"

Rachel answered, "Yeah, it will help you to understand, and not make the same mistakes with other people. But nobody can make you do it. You have to want to."

Ginny came to the heart of the matter when she asked Rachel, "You don't care for Ginny to like Daniel?"

Michael sensed that Rachel would appreciate some help, so he stood by her side and said, "Ginny, it's not that Rachel minds you and Daniel liking each other, she just wants all of you to be safe, and she knows there are a lot of new rules now. She wants to make sure you understand them, like you understood the rules that kept you safe in the woods. It took a while to learn those, too, didn't it?"

William and Ginny both nodded. Rachel breathed a sigh of relief and squeezed Michael's arm in a silent thank you.

As they walked hand in hand to Michael's house, Rachel suddenly giggled, "Poor Pops!"

Michael looked at her and grinned, "Why do you say that?"

"Well, he's the bishop ain't he?" Rachel giggled again.

Michael suddenly looked weary, but still managed a small laugh, "I see your point."

Rachel studied him for a minute and guessed, "You're going to be the next bishop aren't you?"

"I think so," Michael answered. "Pops has been the bishop for almost eight years now. He's tired. He's talked to me a lot lately about being released and how I need to learn all I can. It's not up to him, of course, but Pops knows a lot. He's an inspired man, and his shoes are going to be big ones to fill."

Rachel felt Michael tense up and knew this had to be important to him. "You'll be a good one. How do you feel about it?" Rachel asked.

"I'm really honored, but scared too." Michael squeezed Rachel's hand and relaxed a little, "But now that I'm engaged to my beautiful woman, I'm not nearly as scared anymore."

Rachel smiled her happiness and her stomach fluttered as the enormity of it settled in. She was going to be Michael's wife!

She was only allowed to enjoy the wonderful sensation for a moment. Just as they approached Michael's house, Sarah and Ben joined them and the four of them walked into the house together. Mama and Pops were sitting in the living room in their pajamas. As they removed their coats and hung them up, Pops surveyed the four shining faces and realized this was no ordinary visit. He looked over at Mama and knew she saw it too. She was the first to speak, "Well, look who's here! Would you all like a hot cup of cocoa or herb tea?"

Everybody said they would love it, and went for the hot cocoa that Mama rarely offered. It was in short supply and wouldn't likely be replaced once it was gone.

It was only minutes before they were sitting around the table in the living room sipping the steaming cups of cocoa. They passed the time making small talk, but the strange smiles and conspiring looks kept flying alternately between Sarah and Ben, then Rachel and Michael, followed by questioning looks passing between Mama and Pops. Finally, Pops couldn't stand it anymore, so he demanded, "All right! Out with it. What's going on?" He looked from one couple to the other.

It took a moment for the shock to end and for the smiles

to set in. Everyone knew and appreciated Pops sense of humor and straightforward way, but everyone was a little on edge tonight. Suddenly, Michael and Ben blurted at the same time, "We're getting married!"

Mama raised both hands to her face and squealed, "Oh, my! Both of you? That's wonderful! She hugged Rachel and then Sarah."

Pops slapped the boys on the shoulders and asked, "You didn't really expect me to be surprised did you?" Then he hooted and added, "Fine choices! These ladies won't have any problem keeping you boys straight."

They all took turns congratulating and hugging until they all collapsed on the sofas. Just as it quieted down, a little knock sounded and Pops went to open the door. His eyebrow came to a steep peak when he saw Daniel and Ginny there holding hands. Daniel was shifting nervously from one foot to the other, and Ginny was grinning brightly.

Daniel stammered, "We thought we'd come and tell you...well, is Rachel here? We thought we saw her come in and...."

Ginny helped him out, "Daniel and Ginny courting now. Is good?"

Pops grinned, "Well, this is the night for love! Come on in here and tell Mama so she can squeal again!" He dragged a relieved Daniel into the warmth of his home.

After Ginny blurted her news to everyone, Ben was the first to congratulate, "Go, Daniel boy!" Then it seemed to dawn on him that something was terribly wrong here, and asked with round, alarmed eyes, "Is William going to kill you?"

When Ginny started to go into detail as she had in the greenhouse earlier, Michael broke in, "No! William and Ginny have decided that they just want to be friends now, so William is fine with Ginny having a beau." Michael gave everyone a full, white grin after he looked at Rachel and she mouthed a thank you.

Just as Mama got up to go get two more cups of cocoa,

another knock sounded at the door, so she just stopped in her tracks and giggled, "Well see who else is coming to the love boat, Herbert!"

Pops just slapped his knee and hooted when he opened the door and saw William standing there with the pretty widow Mary Kate. Mama saw poor Mary Kate go pale and ran to the rescue. She pushed Pops aside, who was still grinning, and took Mary Kate by the hand and pulled her inside saying, "You two come right in here and join in the fun. We're so glad you came. You'll just have to excuse our pajamas."

Pops looked down at his pajamas he'd forgotten he had on, and started hooting again. This time everyone else joined in and it truly began to sound like a party.

Mary Kate looked at William with trepidation, but visibly relaxed when he gave her his usual happy smile and told everyone in the room, "Mary Kate and me have been becoming good friends for weeks now 'cause her little boy, Joshua, comes to talk to me all the time in the barn 'cause we both love the animals. Anyhow, he told me he had a real pretty mama one day,...and I reckon he's real right about that!" Everybody laughed and Ben whistled, so William continued, "So now that me and Ginny have things worked out, Mary Kate and me are goin' to court now. Ain't that just real fine?"

Another complete round of hugs and shoulder slaps ensued after the two engagements were announced again. Things had just begun to quiet down when yet another knock sounded at the love-boat hatch. Pops made a big show of counting on his fingers, then announcing, "Well, I don't have any more children left to marry off, so who do you reckon that is?" The group was still laughing quietly when Pops opened the door to a big green Christmas tree.

Pops was feeling quite silly and filled with happiness for his children, so he parted the limbs and called, "Come out, come out, whoever you are, and join us in the love boat!"

If he was shocked to see Joe appear out of the tree, Pops hid it well. He spoke gleefully, "Well, Joe! Come in and join us."

Joe looked warily behind him, and moved a little to the left so Troy could be seen behind the tree. When Pops waited expectantly, Troy finally spoke, "We was all by ourselves back at the house, so we just thought maybe Mama would like to have this here tree we been tendin' to for Christmas." He looked at Joe sheepishly and waited.

Mama rushed to the rescue again and exclaimed, "My goodness! It's a beautiful tree. I didn't know we had any like it around! Please bring it in." Her eyes suddenly widened and she turned to the others sitting around the living room. "I've just hatched a fine idea! Why don't we all go down to Rachel's house and trim the tree together! Rachel, honey, can we hold Christmas celebrations at your house this year since it's big enough to hold us all?"

Rachel looked at Michael and saw how pleased he was that Mama had asked, so she beamed the approval that had begun to fill her heart, "That would be great! Can we go now? It could be like a big engagement celebration!"

Troy asked amid the fray in the room, "So you finally got your man, Rachel?" He suddenly looked embarrassed that he had asked the question, but Ben surged to the rescue.

"Not only did Rachel snag Michael, but I'm happy to say I've been snagged, too! We're all getting married!" Ben grinned so broadly that Sarah felt compelled to punch him in the chest.

Joe looked at Daniel and Ginny holding hands, then at Mary Kate and William, and spouted, "Got anybody in mind for me and Troy?"

The silence only lasted for a second before the whole room erupted in laughter again. Then Pops looked at Joe with eyes filled with acceptance and promised, "You just hang around long enough, young man, there's love in the air in Rocktown Village. It's bound to get you!"

Epilogue
One Year Later

Rachel watched as everybody put Christmas ornaments on the tree that Troy and Joe had come up with again this year. It wasn't nearly as pretty and perfect as the one last year, but it was miraculous that they had one at all. A gallant effort was being put forth to enjoy the occasion, but something was about to happen, and it hung thick in the air. It was impossible to concentrate on anything else.

Michael caught Rachel's eye and smiled. She smiled in return, but in truth could only think of how different this Christmas season was from the last. She and Michael had gotten married in April, he had been called to be the bishop in May, and the months spent with him had been the happiest in her life. She touched her stomach and smiled as she thought of Michael's child growing within her. They would have a little baby that looked like them in the spring.

Troy had been there to give her away. He told her later that it had been the most important moment in his life. He had finally asked Pops and Michael to give him a blessing to heal the nerve damage that was far more serious than he had ever admitted. He was doing fine now, said he was fit as a fiddle. He had started referring to himself as Grandpa.

Daniel and Ginny were still very fond of each other in that very special way, but as they had been counseled, were giving themselves plenty of time to grow and even date other people. William and Mary Kate had gotten married just two months after Rachel and Michael had, and Joe had a girlfriend. He had just confided in Michael and Rachel that he planned on asking her to marry him when he could take her to the temple. Adam and Christina had a beautiful baby girl named Hope who had indeed sweetened a bitter time. Sarah and Ben's wedding date was set for early in the spring.

In the spring. That was such a strange thought now. The spring would not be as any other spring had ever been on the earth. By then everything would be different. She thought how quickly things had changed after she and Michael were married. Instead of the days getting longer as they normally did for the summer months, they had started getting shorter. The sun shone less and less everyday, until now they were lucky to get a few hours of light each day. It was 3:00 o'clock in the afternoon and it was dark outside.

Michael attended meetings at the Church headquarters about twenty miles away every week, sometimes several times a week, to keep himself and his people informed and prepared. Everything had changed so suddenly. Just when it seemed that life was even and steady in Rocktown Village, they got the news that they needed to stockpile all available supplies and food as quickly as possible. They were assured there would be no more people moving between villages and that there would be no more new converts.

Anyone able to work labored night and day to harvest and preserve the last of the greenhouse and the stocking field's produce. Michael and Pops led the effort to slaughter all of the stock animals in the barn. William had cried when he was informed that many of the animals he had become quite attached to would be slaughtered. Mama, Pops and Ben moved into the big house with Michael and Rachel to conserve resources.

Conditions worsened steadily after that. Everyone was ready physically, and they met often as a whole village to uplift themselves spiritually. Rachel was so proud of Michael and what a wonderful leader he was. Oftentimes, the people would ask him to speak to them even though he had assigned others to speak. The words that flowed so freely from his mouth came straight from his heart, and Rachel never failed to find comfort and new understanding in his words.

News traveled to them regularly now about the many wars that raged around the world, particularly in Israel. Occasionally, they could pick up a station on the hand-cranked radio that spelled out how devastating and total the destruction really was. Sometimes they could see strange lights in the sky far away and they each knew in their heart what it meant. But there still wasn't any international travel. The sea and sky around the country had kept it isolated for years with their vicious winds and waves. They counted it as another blessing from God since it kept their sons at home, away from the raging wars abroad.

The cries and unrest had become vicious outside the village walls in the last few weeks. Rachel quivered when she thought of what it would be like if she and the band were still trapped out there. No wonder the people screamed and cried outside the walls, she was sure there was no comfort to be found.

The elements had been unpredictable for years, as far back as the first time she left Minnesota, back when Michael and his family had moved to the village. But none of them could have imagined how much worse it would become. Now it was apparent that the earth refused to function. All things were out of order, preparing for the new order. There was no longer the night and the day, the cold and the hot, or the wet and the dry. It was as though they had all become one, all muffled and broken. A dark mist hung over the earth that made it hard to even breathe at times. It gave the appearance of having moisture, yet the earth was strangely parched. Even those who sat waiting, prepared, could find no rest.

Rachel walked away from the tree and the group quietly hanging the ornaments and thought how strange it was that they were celebrating His birth. She stared out the window at the moon that had appeared with its eerie red tinge swirling about it, ebbing in and out of the thick, black clouds that were ever-present these days. Somehow, Rachel knew the sun was still out there, masking its face, though she couldn't really see it directly.

It was as though it sadly testified of the blood that was being shed around the world by its reflection through the moon, the lesser light. She wondered again, as she had a million times before, how it would be when He came. She had listened closely to all that Michael and the others had said. She had studied long hours from the scriptures, yet the uneasiness continued.

As though they were giving voice to her thoughts, she heard the twins behind her ask Michael, "Uncle Michael, will you do something for us?" Amy pleaded.

Michael smiled at them and said, "Sure. What is it?"

Paul answered, "Will you sit down with us and tell us what it is really going to be like when Jesus comes? We've listened to all the sermons, well most of them anyway, but it's not a whole story."

Amy added, "And we keep making up things to fill in the holes, and now we're really scared. But we want to know the truth, even if it's scary."

Jeremy came running over and surprised everyone when he said quite seriously, "Me, too, Uncle Michael. Tell me the whole story, so I won't be so scared."

Michael immediately looked to Adam and Christina and received a nod from Adam and a smile of appreciation from Christina. "Okay, you bet I will. Come on over here and let's sit on the rug in front of the fireplace together." Michael suddenly realized why The Coming had been playing in his mind like a movie on a screen for days.

William followed them and asked quietly, "Is it okay if I listen too, Michael?"

Before Michael could answer, Ginny and Sarah joined them and Sarah added, "Us, too."

Michael watched in quiet respect as everyone in the room dropped their ornaments, including Pops and Mama, and gathered around on the floor or on the sofas. Everyone knew what he was doing when Michael lowered his eyes and sat quietly for a minute before he began. Then he smiled at everyone, looked directly at the twins and said, "I'm going to tell you about the greatest event that will ever happen to mankind. Do you know why Jesus's coming back to the earth again is even more wonderful than his birth was?"

When Amy and Paul shook their heads, Michael continued, "Well, for the first time ever, every person will finally recognize that he is Jesus and bow down to him.

"Even though it seems scary for you right now, Jesus had to let it get this bad. He had to let everybody choose, whether they'd choose good or bad. Some people have followed what he said to do, and he wants to bless them. But, the truth is, most of the people have chosen to do really bad things and have not loved him and his teachings, and he must punish them as he has warned over and over again, or he would not be a fair God. Do you understand?" When the twins and Jeremy nodded their heads, Michael continued.

"Every one of us knew it would be hard when we came here for this earth life. Sometimes it would even be very confusing. But Jesus gave us everything we needed to learn about him and his teachings. Only those teachings can make us happy and keep us safe. Nothing else will work. He gave us the scriptures, he gave us parents, and missionaries, and church leaders. The message has gone throughout the whole world and people everywhere have had the chance to love him. But you can never make someone else love you. They have to choose to love you. Jesus knew that, so he has let us choose."

Jeremy interrupted, "I love Jesus, Uncle Michael."

Michael smiled, "I know you do, Jeremy, and he knows you do because you remember him. A lot of people say they love him, but then they don't do anything to prove they really do love him. You prove it when you pray everyday, when you take care of your body and don't take anything into it that will hurt it. When you go to church and share everything that you have with the poor and because you have done these things, and many others, you will be safe and will not be punished when Jesus comes to punish the wicked."

"Why did it have to be like this, Michael? It just seems

so mean and sad," Amy appealed. "Everything is so messed up. I'm scared."

Michael took a deep breath, fully understanding his little niece's heartache and fear, then plunged right in. "Amy, you know that we lived with Heavenly Father as his spirit children before we came to the earth, just like Jesus did, right? Well, Heavenly Father knew that we couldn't become as good and wise as we could be, like Him, if we never got a chance to prove we would be true and faithful when we were away from him. If he had controlled everything, it would be like your Mommy keeping you in the house all the time just because she didn't want you to do anything wrong or get hurt."

Amy thought about that for a minute and said, "Okay, that makes sense. But Mommy would never let me play outside all night until I hurt myself. She would just make me stop. Why don't Jesus just make this all stop, because I hear people crying?"

"That's exactly what he's going to do, Amy. He's given everybody plenty of time to make their choices, and now he's going to stop it just like he said he would. I know it feels like it's been too long and too hard, but Heavenly Father wanted to make sure he'd found every last child of his that would listen and love him before he told Jesus it was time to come and stop it. What if Rachel hadn't taken the time to go and find Jeremy when he was lost? See, Jesus loves every single one of the people out there just like we love Jeremy, and he wanted to find every last one of them."

The point was well made when Joe offered, "I'm real glad he gave me a little more time."

Paul grinned at Joe who had become his good friend and said, "Me too!" Then he became solemn again as he asked, "If Jesus loves everybody, then how can he stand destroying them, even if they have been bad? Mommy and Daddy don't destroy us when we are bad."

"Well, first of all, Jesus would never destroy little children no matter what, because they are innocent, and he would never destroy anybody that would love him even just a little bit, because anybody that loves Jesus, also loves other people, and that is really what Jesus wants from us. He might not give them as big a reward as he would somebody who loved him and other people a whole lot, but he would never destroy them. Paul, do you remember when the wolverine took Jeremy?"

Paul's eyes grew large and exclaimed, "Yeah, and I would've killed him myself if Rachel hadn't got him."

Michael asked, "Why would you have *destroyed* him, Paul?"

Paul didn't miss the use of that word, he looked at Amy and silently they shared their understanding. Paul answered, "Because he was hurting Jeremy and I love Jeremy."

Michael looked at Naomi and knew it was a difficult question he would ask her, but also knew it needed to be asked. "Naomi, how do you feel about the people who tried to kill Peter when he only wanted to save them by teaching them about Jesus?"

Naomi looked shocked for a moment, wondering how Michael could know how angry she had been over that very thing, how he could know how confused and hurt she was over the suffering that went on right outside the village gates. She suddenly realized how she had been blaming God for letting it get out of control. She sighed and admitted, "I feel like they should be destroyed if they will not stop doing things like that, because I love Peter very much."

Michael smiled and said, "Exactly. Jesus will not destroy the wicked because he is mean, but because he is good, just and fair. He cannot let them go on hurting other people, and it always hurts other people in one way or the other if someone is wicked."

William asked, "But why is the earth goin' so crazy? It seems like everybody, even those that aren't wicked or hurting anybody else, are gonna get destroyed, too."

"I'm getting ready to tell you the whole story now, of what it will really be like, and how you will be safe. But let me tell you about the earth first. You all know that Heavenly Father told Jesus Christ to create this earth, this world, just for us. It took him a long time, too. He didn't just throw any old thing together. He created something really wonderful for us, something so beautiful and special. He made great hills and valleys, mountains, lakes and streams and rushing rivers. He made the seas and oceans and every kind of living thing to supply our needs and wants for comfort and joy. Ben, do you remember that model you made of the farm when you were in junior high school?"

Ben grinned and said, "Yeah, I remember. I worked for weeks on that thing!" He looked at Sarah and laughed, "I was so picky about it, just like I am about all of my models, that I gave a whole week's allowance to Michael to take me to a bigger town fifty miles away just so I could get the exact right color of paint that matched the color on our house. It took me three days to paint it because I kept getting the white shutter paint on the green house paint."

Sarah injected, "You aren't tellin' me anything! Remember, I was there when Rachel nearly threw your model car at Michael, and you still turned white when Pops teased you about it later."

Ben shrugged, "I take my model building seriously."

Michael picked up the story, "Well, Jesus takes his earth-building seriously, too, and he is happy for people to use it for what it was intended for, but is not happy at all when people misuse it. See, Ben loved for people to look at his model farm and enjoy all of the intricate detail and hard work he put into it because that is why he made it, and he knew the people were grateful when they were careful not to knock any of the little trees or buildings over, or spill things on it. But you should have seen him when Naomi let our little cousins play with it in her room!"

Everybody laughed and Naomi defended, "Hey, I had to give him my whole week's allowance to buy new paint just because it had a few scratches on it!"

Michael waited for them to quiet down, then asked the

question, "Ben, what did you do with your model after that?"

Ben answered, "I took it back! Naomi thought it looked really cool on her shelf and asked me if she could keep it. When she didn't take care of it, I felt betrayed and took it back to my room."

Naomi stuck her tongue out at Ben which started a whole new round of laughter, but everybody settled down quickly when Michael cleared his throat and said, "That's what Jesus is about to do with the earth. He made it with great care and intended for people to learn and grow and have joy in it. But they have defiled it—that means they didn't take care of it after Jesus trusted them with it. It doesn't work right anymore, either, because Jesus has withdrawn his light and spirit from it, and that's what made it so beautiful and good in the first place. Everything on the earth, besides the gathered people who are good and honest, has become very wicked, so Jesus is going to take it back."

Amy said, "I'm glad Jesus is going to take it back, Uncle Michael. He must be very sad that his beautiful earth has been de...defiled. Where will he put it, Uncle Michael? It is so big, how will he take it?"

Michael smiled, "He's not going to move it anywhere, like Ben moved his model, he's just going to come here to Earth and take it back from the wicked people by ruling and reigning himself. Then he's going to let the righteous people live on it and be their leader for a long time, for a thousand years. The earth will be wonderful and much more beautiful and perfect than it ever was before.

"But some serious things have to happen first. Here is how it will go. First, things are going to get worse, it will get darker and you'll hear even more terrible sounds out there." As if to demonstrate, the sky released several seconds of vicious, loud thundering and lightnings, but Michael continued. "Then Jesus will come to the Valley of Adam-ondi-Ahman, right here in Jackson County, and visit the resurrected Adam and all the holy men, including the prophet and many of the leaders in the Church right now. He will show his face to them first because they have loved him and kept his commandments, and they need to give back to Jesus all the keys and authority he has given them, so he will be the rightful leader and Lord over all the earth. He will tell us and teach us anything else we need to know to be safe while the wicked are being destroyed."

"Gosh, will you be there, Uncle Michael!" exclaimed Paul.

"I really hope so, Paul. It would be the greatest honor of my life, but if I'm not there it's okay, because all of the good people will see him soon after that anyway. Jesus will come down out of the sky so the whole world can see and hear him all at the same time. His voice will be like thunder and everyone will see his face like the sun in the sky.

"All of those that have been gathered will be happy and will rejoice when they see his face and hear his voice. They will be happy to kneel before him and honor him because that will mean the darkness is almost over. But there will be some who have not loved him and kept his commandments, and they will be full of sorrow and mourning because they know they have not prepared, yet they will kneel at his feet and ask him to forgive them. I will tell you more about them in just a minute.

"Then there will be many who are Jesus's enemies, the wicked. They have knowingly fought against him and his people, like the ones who tried to kill Peter. They will hear Jesus's voice of thunder and see his face like the sun, but you know what?"

All three of the children and William asked at the same time, "What?"

"They will just stand there against Jesus, even though they know he can destroy them, until he shakes the earth and causes them to fall at his feet." Michael paused a minute to catch his breath. It was as though he was living the events right now, and wondered if it felt that way to anyone else.

"Then Jesus will lift up and separate all of those who have willingly bowed before him and called him Lord, from those who are wicked and have fallen to their knees. He has to destroy the wicked, but he does not want the righteous to have to see the sorrow and destruction, so that is why they will be lifted up and away so they won't have to look. It's important that you realize Jesus will not enjoy destroying the wicked, it has already brought him great sorrow that he has to do such a thing. But the right must win."

Jeremy had been listening intently and spoke very quietly, reverently, "Uncle Michael, I'm glad I won't have to watch. I didn't watch when Rachel destroyed the monster and...and she cried because she had to do it."

Michael looked at Rachel with all of the deep love and respect she deserved, then confirmed to Jeremy and the other children, "That is exactly right, Jeremy. I am so very proud of how well you children are listening and understanding. Jesus is proud of you, too." Each child nodded and looked proud of themselves, but not nearly as proud as Adam and Christina looked.

Smiling, Michael continued, "After Jesus has cleansed the earth of the wicked, then he will again set those he has saved back down on the earth to live with him where he will reign in a world of peace for a thousand years."

Michael waited for a minute to let it all sink in and asked if anyone had any questions so far. Then he said, "There are two more things I want to tell you about. Does anybody know what that one thousand years with Jesus is called?"

Troy was the one to amaze everyone this time when he answered quietly, "It's called the millennium." When everyone just sat silently after he said that, he felt like he had time to ask the question that burned in his heart, "There's somethin' that's really bothering me, though. You see, my patriarchal blessing that I got last month told me that I am from the tribe of Judah." He looked down with a kind of shame and finished, "I am a Jew."

Michael was quick to dispel that shame, "Then you are of God's chosen house. That is the second thing I wanted to tell you about, but just let me say a couple of things about the millennium first. "It is important to understand that the thousand years, the millennium, is to get us ready to live in heaven, because you see, according to Jesus, no person has ever entered into that wonderful place without first completing his millennial probation. When it is over, then the final judgement day will come and everybody will receive their just reward for time and all eternity. They will enter into that life which has no end and no beginning. It's called that because it's a cycle that we are all a part of forever, and we'll be able to see and understand *all* of it then."

He paused to catch his breath and looked at the children, and all of his beloved family with respect, for he knew they had each earned their safety when Christ did come. He thought he would tell them more about the millennium if there was time after he told them about the Jewish people. He understood now why that subject burned in his heart. Troy was Jewish. He would want to know about his lineage of people.

"Okay, do you remember earlier when I told you I'd tell you more about some people who were not prepared when Jesus came, but they would kneel at his feet full of sorrow and mourning? Well, the biggest group of those people are the Jewish people. If you remember, Jesus himself was Jewish, so he deeply loves his people. But he is allowing them, his chosen house, right now, to be chastised one last time for their transgressions, their sins against Him."

Amy interrupted, "Because they crucified him when he was just trying to teach them the truth, like Peter."

"That's right," Michael praised.

Paul asked, "Does chastised mean punished?"

"Yes, Paul it does."

"How is he punishing them right now?" Paul wanted to know.

"Well, there is a terrible war going on right now in Israel, where many of the Jews have gathered. Their enemies are trying to destroy them and have already killed so many.

But as soon as Jesus has allowed them to be chastised this one last time for not recognizing him and not serving him, then he will come in among them and save them from their enemies just as he has promised. Just as he was willing to do so long ago when they would not receive him.

"Their sorrow is going to be very great when they recognize him, when they realize he came to them so long ago and they rejected him. But, he will save his own, for his grace is sufficient for them that love him, even in their sorrow and shame. Those people will be lifted up with the rest of his gathered people, and saved, because they have suffered enough and have paid the price for their sins. Jesus would have borne it all for them if they would have accepted him before."

Everyone sat silently, pondering all that Michael had taught them. Then Joe looked at Michael with his emotions barely held in check and said, "It is sad how stubborn and hard some of us can be. I'm just glad I had all of you to keep helpin' me. I'm sorry I took so long, and I thank you for hangin' onto me."

Pops reached out from where he sat and put a big hand firmly on Joe's shoulder and squeezed his approval, and his acceptance of his thanks. Michael verbalized, "It is sad, Joe. It's part of the tension and pain we feel right now, even though we sit here prepared. There are still so many who will not humble themselves before Jesus, and that is why his righteous indignation, his anger, is full. Even in this very day when darkness rules and all is lost except the gathered from among the people, the wicked still stand and sneer and say that He is not."

* * * *

Rachel snuggled into Michael's shoulder and felt at peace. It was late, and Michael had just returned from a conference with the Prophet and other church leaders. Something had come over their whole family after Michael had finished with the story of Christ's second coming yesterday. A peace. An acceptance. A feeling of unity and calmness. They had all prayed together and that's when it had happened, and it had been with each one of them since.

Michael raised her chin to look at him and asked, "How are you feeling, and the baby?"

Rachel propped herself on the pillow so she could look at Michael as she talked, but they continued to hold hands beneath the covers. "We feel great," she smiled.

Michael could barely contain his happiness. He was always so thankful to return home to Rachel. He looked forward to every minute he could spend with her and the baby. He reverently placed his hand on her belly and smiled with satisfaction when the baby moved for him. He looked at Rachel with all the wonder that filled his soul, and asked, "Has she moved a lot today?"

"Oh! It is a she, huh?" Rachel laughed.

Michael answered honestly, "I think so. Do you?"

"Yeah, I guess that's what I think, too. Is that okay with you?"

"It's perfect with me," Michael stated. "Have you thought of a special name yet?"

She was sure they had examined every name that ever existed for a boy or a girl, but there was one she favored, that kept coming to her mind again and again. "Well...there is one, if it's a girl."

Michael looked round eyed with excitement when he demanded, "Tell me!"

Rachel laughed at his enthusiasm, and loved him all the more for it. "Maggie. After Mama."

Michael smiled his approval and said, "She'll squeak for a week when you tell her!"

They fell silent when the noise and darkness intruded on them from outside. The rumblings and roaring had been so loud the last two days that no one even went outside unless they had to. It could turn dark or light, spit hail or snow, dribble or pour, from one minute to the next. The endless waiting was taking it's toll on everyone.

Michael continued with his hand on Rachel's stomach, continued to feel the life there. It brought him an odd kind of peace, of hope, a purpose more complete than any he'd known. Maggie.

When he felt Rachel tense from the next loud crack that split the sky, he offered, "Want to talk about Maggie?"

Rachel smiled, and welcomed the diversion. "Sure. Tell me about Maggie."

Michael began, "Maggie will have a wonderful world to grow up in. By the time she gets to us here on earth, it will be all clean and peaceful. The elements will operate in perfect order, just like they did in the Garden of Eden in the beginning. Can you see the lamb and the lion lying down together, honey? Can you see a world full of people who are all honest and fair with each other?"

Rachel was beginning to see, to be drawn into Michael's vision. She snuggled closer and acknowledged, "Mmmm. Tell me more."

"The continents will be brought back together again into one beautiful, complete land. It will be one world government with a perfect order ruled over by a perfect leader. No more wars, no more killing or dying. There will be two world capitals, one in Jerusalem and the other here in Missouri. We'll all be one people, living together in peace, raising our families. Raising Maggie."

Rachel asked, "Where will we live, Michael?"

"Anywhere we want to, honey. We can ask for a farm to raise Maggie on, or we could live here or in Jerusalem and live a life in the hum of a city in government work. It's up to us. There will always be free choice when God is in control, and it will be fair, there will be no poor among us."

Rachel smiled a little more than she had in weeks. "Tell me more."

"Maggie will be able to plant her own little garden and will get only sweet, good things for her efforts. The earth won't even bring forth briars or thistles or anything bad anymore. Each family will build their own home for themselves and their labors will be for their own family from their own hands." Michael paused. "We got so far away from that in this world, Rachel."

"Will it ever get like this again?" Rachel worried.

"No. Maggie will never have to see it like this. Oh, toward the end of the millennium some will start to turn away again, because there will be many born during the thousand years and all will still have their free agency to choose. Some will even choose to follow Satan when he's set free one last time at the end of the Millennium. But with Jesus in leadership, it will never spiral out of control again. He will not permit it.

"It will be a long-awaited time of peace and joy upon the earth. The people will not be perfect, but in the worst, they will be good and honest people, and in the best, they will be ready for heaven or the Celestial Kingdom. All of the good people who have ever lived and passed on will come back and live with us as resurrected beings. The wicked will have to wait in spirit prison until the end of the Millennium to be resurrected and given their final assignment."

"Grandmaw Bentley could be here, to be with Maggie?" Rachel marveled.

"It is definitely possible, if she has earned the first resurrection." Michael's eyes lit up with his next thought, "Oh, honey, wait until you meet Grandmother Rock! I loved her so much, and she was such a good and kind woman. Maggie is going to be crazy about her! And she won't even be old or in pain like she was when I knew her. She had arthritis. And Grandfather Rock! He hoots more than Pops! I can't wait to see them again."

"How will we find them, Michael? Where will they be? I want to find them right away," Rachel exclaimed with so much joy at the prospect of meeting them. She loved old people best of all.

Michael laughed out loud at her enthusiasm. Neither of them even noticed the increased activity outside. "Well, I don't have all of the answers, but I suspect we'll be close to all of the people we love when we are gathered there in the sky. I can't think of anything that would distract from what is going on below any better than seeing loved ones that have passed on for the first time again. That would bring a lot of joy, and we are supposed to have joy when He comes, so that could explain how it would happen while all of that destruction is going on below."

"It sounds right, Michael. We have a lot to look forward to with Maggie. I love you, Michael, and I love Maggie."

Michael had gone silent, and as Rachel listened, she knew why.

It was time.

Pops knocked on their bedroom door just as Michael was getting dressed. He called softly through the door, "It's time, son. They've sent for you to come to the valley."

Michael looked at Rachel and saw that she wasn't scared, but came to her and implored, "We are ready, right?"

"Just like you promised, Michael. Just like you promised."

And the Seventh Angel sounded; and there were great voices in heaven, saying, the kingdoms of this world are become the Kingdom of our Lord, and of His Christ; and He shall reign for ever and ever. (Revelation 11:15)

Biography

Vickie Mason Randalls is a graduate of Virginia Intermont College with degrees in Journalism and Horsemanship.

Vickie's writing career began with the campus newspaper as a staff writer, where she authored several full-length feature stories. She has been published in *Scouting* magazine with articles in their *Family Talk* feature column.

Vickie comes from the Appalachian Mountains in Virginia where she owned and operated a horseback riding academy for many years. She has most recently worked as a district director for the Boy Scouts of America. Vickie is now writing full time, currently working on her second novel in the Earth Phase trilogy.

For the past several years Vickie has enjoyed teaching a four year seminary course designed for the high school youth in her church congregation. The highlight for her has been the prophesies and teachings concerning the second coming of Jesus Christ, adding to her twenty-year search of prophetic history.

Vickie's interests and hobbies include journal writing, walking, TaeKwonDo, self-sufficiency homesteading, genealogical research, reading, and gardening.

Vickie counts her family as her greatest blessing. Vickie and David, her husband of twenty-four years, live in south central Minnesota bordering the Blue Earth River. They are enjoying parenting three children and the three family dogs.

Excerpt for "Rising Sons,"
The second in the "Earth Family" trilogy.

The rustling of the leaves exploded with sound, with sensation so vivid that the man smiled. He lifted his foot and reverently crunched one more time before his attention was drawn to the tiny fawn. It came wobbling, tripping over to him without fear.

The man's face trasformed into a somber, magical stare. He lowered his massive frame to one knee and slowly stretched forth his large, calloused hand and stroked the fawn's tiny neck. It was a tentative, surreal thing at first, then the man picked the baby up full into his embrace. He bowed his head and snuggled its warmth, savoring the milky breath and earthy tones of it.

For six thousand years he had waited—longed for this moment. The moment when his immortal self would connect with his sweet mother earth again. When all enmity had ceased and the reign of the Dark One was finally over. Now he could embrace the long hoped-for peace. It was finally his again. Finally.

She watched silently, hating to interrupt her mate. He looked so peaceful with that little baby deer tucked in his big arms. And she couldn't be sure, but she thought she saw moisture glistening in his eyes. She pushed an errant strand of long dark hair from her face and peered a moment longer—remembering. She recalled a scene so similar, so many millennia ago, when she had first awakened in this very place and found him here.

She looked at her man now with no less appreciation than she had then. He was in every deed a beautiful thing, inside and out. And now, after all this time, the attraction still caught her off guard, making her feel like a giddy, mortal teenager. Before she could stop herself, a giggle of pure joy bubbled up through her and escaped her throat.

The man's head snapped up, and immediately a boyish grin split his face. He gently lowered the fawn to the ground, giving it a nudge toward its waiting mother. He stood to his full towering height and opened his arms toward the woman who stood at the edge of The Garden.